The Sun Rises in the West

Isabel Keats

THE SUN RISES IN THE WEST

Translation: Ian Davis.
Cover & layout design: soniarte.mvg@gmail.com

http://www.isabelkeats.com/
mail to:isabelkeats@gmail.com

In memory of long summer afternoons spent engrossed
in the action-packed stories of Zane Grey and James O. Curwood
that my father collected.
May this novel make you dream, too.

1

The Delta Airlines plane landed abruptly on one of the few runways at Jackson Hole Airport that the snowplows had finished clearing after the previous day's heavy snowfall. The plane slowed to a crawl down the dark runway, and through the fogged glass of the windows I could see the huge mounds of accumulated snow standing out vividly against the wet tarmac.

A short distance away, an airport worker was spraying the fuselage of a huge gray plane with a hose from the small crane of a tanker truck, and although the temperature inside the plane was pleasant, I couldn't help but shiver.

"And I thought I was out of all of this for good," I muttered grumpily.

After the harsh winters of my childhood in Chicago, I had vowed to live in one of those paradisiacal corners that appeared in the back issues of the magazines that my mother, who worked as a janitor in an office building, would bring home at the end of her shift. In these idyllic places where the sun shone at all hours, the temperature was wonderful, and the beaches with transparent water invited you to swim. Finally, my dream had come true. After years of tireless work, I had managed to become a *prima ballerina* with the Los Angeles Ballet, and whenever I could, I would escape with my friends from the company to Venice Beach to take advantage of the little free time we had between performances and rehearsals.

The thought of those happy times made my stomach churn, and I was glad when the plane finally stopped and I had no choice but to attend to more prosaic matters, such as retrieving my suitcase from the crowded baggage compartment. Once I had my suitcase off the conveyor belt, I made my way to the exit with weary steps. Outside, a crowd was waiting impatiently for their loved ones, but no one was waiting for me. As usual, I was surfing on a wave of self-pity. Lately it had become my only sport.

"Miss Brooks?"

At least no one I knew. Surprised, I looked up to see a guy in his early twenties holding a piece of cardboard with my name in capital letters. "Yes, it's me, how did you know?"

"They told me about a girl who was traveling alone, blonde, petite and very attractive." He made a mischievous gesture that made him look even more seductive, but I just stared at him and didn't even smile.

"Are you Vance Bennet?" But before I even finished, I realized that this stranger was too young to be Raff's friend.

He cleared his throat and continued in a more serious tone, "I'm Josh, his brother. Vance couldn't make it, there's a lot going on at the ranch getting ready for spring calving, and he's the one in charge."

I didn't ask what he meant. For a while now, most things mattered little to me. My curiosity was dead and I didn't feel the slightest interest in the place where, against my will, I was forced to spend the next few months. I had barely noticed the Jackson airport, built of wood and stone and full of cozily lit fireplaces, although it was one of the most charming I had ever been to. I realized that the young beardless boy was still talking nonstop. Apparently, my silence was making him nervous, and the thought almost made me smile for the first time in months.

"I came in the pickup, it's not a very luxurious means of transportation, but with yesterday's rain, it's the most practical. May I?", he pointed to the wheeled suitcase next to me.

I shrugged and, without even thanking him, began to walk at a brisk pace – although walking would be too strong a word; with my limp, it would be more like a graceless trot – toward the exit. My hostile attitude must have surprised him, because this Josh guy froze for a few seconds before grabbing the handle of the suitcase and following me in a hurry.

As soon as I stepped outside, a blast of icy wind with a good load of compact flakes hit me in the face. Shivering, I bundled up in the leather jacket I had bought before coming, which was clearly inadequate for the frigid Wyoming winter. Josh didn't miss my gesture and hurried to open the door of a beat-up pickup truck with huge snow tires. "That coat's too thin and your boots aren't right either, don't you have any others?"

"No. I came from Los Angeles and these were the warmest things I could find. Would you mind closing the door, I'm freezing?"

"Sorry", embarrassed, he shut the door tightly, loaded the suitcase into the tarp-covered bed, and hurried into the pickup. He started the engine, turned the heater on full blast, and pulled into the driveway. "So Los Angeles, huh?"

It was obvious that Josh was not one to give up easily. Chances were his brother Vance – one of my brother's best friends since college days – had filled him in on the juicy details of my sob story. I could almost picture those pretty gray eyes watering with tears as he listened to how my promising dance career had been cut short by a stupid car accident. Surely the poor guy had decided that it was normal for me to be less than friendly under the circumstances and was determined to be extremely patient with me.

"No wonder you're freezing, it's five degrees below zero. What was the temperature there?"

"I didn't bother to find out." I noticed that he looked at me sideways. Despite all the chatter at the airport about a petite, attractive blonde girl, I had no doubt that at that moment he felt he had overdone it. I was the first to know how much my physical appearance had deteriorated in recent times. For one thing, I was too thin. My face was haggard, and deep dark circles under my eyes made my brown eyes look as big as those of poor African children with swollen bellies. My hair, though an unusual shade of light blonde, had lost its luster, and I wore it pulled back in an ungraceful bun anyway. And though I came from sunny California, my skin was pale and unhealthy.

The clothes I was wearing didn't suit me either. Apart from the old-fashioned leather jacket – which didn't keep me warm enough and which I'd bought at a flea market at a bargain price – I'd lost too much weight in the last few months and my dark pants were several sizes too big. The truth was, I didn't care in the least, and that's why I hadn't bothered to update my wardrobe. I no longer remembered the times when men turned around when I walked by.

"I drive slowly because the snowplows can't keep up and there's still a lot of clearing to do, but the Double B isn't more than twenty-five miles from Jackson." For the next minutes, my companion talked incessantly about the ranch, the cattle, the weather, the most amusing places in town… Apparently my lack of response and the fact that I kept looking out the window without paying the slightest attention to him added to his communicative zeal.

The landscape was a dull duotone; the immaculate white of the snow that covered the meadows contrasted with the gray of the trunks and bare branches of the frost-covered trees. I watched the panorama with indifference until, on the other side of the wooden fence that separated the fields from the road, a moving patch of color suddenly broke the monotony.

A herd of horses, their coats ranging from pale gold to dark brown, came out of nowhere and galloped for quite a while in friendly competition with the truck, their long manes blowing in the wind. I had never seen such a spectacle outside of a movie theater, and I could not suppress an exclamation of delight, "Did you see that?" I pointed at the magnificent animals in wonder as my lips curled into an involuntary smile.

Josh stared at me. It had been so long since I had smiled that I had apparently forgotten the effect that simple gesture used to have on teachers, classmates, and even my brother Raff. Seeing his shocked expression, I pressed my lips tightly together, determined to become the unfriendly little bitch he had greeted at the airport.

Just then, we passed under a wooden archway that read "Double B Ranch". Two intertwined B's hung from a chain, and my expansive companion began another of those long explanations he was so fond of.

"This is the entrance to the Double B," he said needlessly. "You see that symbol? That's the iron brand of our cattle. We breed some of the finest Quarter Horses in the country." A tinge of pride vibrated in his words. "We must have about five hundred right now, although the Double B's specialty is beef cattle, fed almost exclusively on pasture. We have about four thousand head, mostly Black Angus and…"

"Would you mind not talking for a while? I have a headache."

"Yeah? Poor thing, I'm sorry."

His kind tone made me roll my eyes. Apparently the whippersnapper was impervious to bad manners.

"As soon as we get home, I'll get you some Tylenol or something, but don't worry, I'll keep my mouth shut." True to his word, he spent the rest of the ride humming a tune with pounding insistence. He broke his silence only when he stopped the pickup in front of a large wooden building and announced enthusiastically: "Welcome to the Double B, Miss Brooks!"

A few minutes later, my suitcase and I found ourselves in the middle of a huge double-height room with a ceiling of massive exposed wooden beams. This time I looked around curiously, and much to my regret I had to admit that the interior of the house was just as impressive as the exterior.

In the floor-to-ceiling rustic stone fireplace, the fire glowed deliciously cozy against the snowy landscape shown through the wide windows that flanked it. In front of it, three aged leather couches, sized to match the rest of the room, invited conversation. The floor of wide, rough-hewn wooden planks was almost entirely covered in fluffy, long-haired rugs. I was about to let out a whistle that was anything but ladylike. The place looked like the set of a cowboy movie, albeit a movie about filthy rich cowboys.

"Mom, our guest is here!" Josh called. Immediately, a red-haired head peeked over the wooden railing that connected the room to the upstairs, and a pair of inquisitive eyes scanned me, making no attempt to hide their curiosity.

"Carol, tell mother!" Without a word, the young girl ran to obey him.

Five minutes later, a very beautiful woman of about fifty years of age appeared in the room, accompanied by the teenage girl. Both were tall and slender, with hair of a very similar reddish-golden hue, though one wore it loose at shoulder length and the other pulled back in a braid that almost reached her waist. Both had the same gray eyes as Josh, and it wasn't hard to guess that they were mother, daughter, and brother.

"Welcome, Aisha, isn't it? I'm Tessa." The woman held out her hand with a languid air.

"Aisha Brooks, indeed." I shook her hand firmly and watched with malicious satisfaction as she pursed her lips in an almost imperceptible grimace of pain.

"I'm Carol Bennet," the teenager held out her hand in return, but her grip was tighter and I couldn't repeat the move. "May we call you by your first name?"

"Of course. And since we're all friends now," I used my most insolent tone, "I'd like to talk to Vance. ASAP."

The woman's gray eyes narrowed, but she replied politely, "My son is very busy at the moment, you can see him at dinner time."

Her words made me frown. "Vance is your son? I thought he was the same age as my brother Raff."

"Actually, he's my stepson, I married his father when Vance was Carol's age. But from what he told us, you and Raff aren't blood-related either, am I right?"

Yes, she was right, but I didn't like being reminded of it. To me, Raff was as much my brother as if the same woman had given birth to us. My father had been living with Raff's mother for some time, and one fine day – I was about six years old – he took off, leaving me like an old piece of junk, with an out-of-tune harmonica and a few patched clothes for my entire fortune.

Raff's mother wasn't exactly swimming in riches on her janitor's salary. But she took me in like a daughter, and none of them ever made me feel like I was superfluous to the family. And though Raff was not at the top of my popularity list at the moment – after all, that obnoxious protective spirit that characterized him was responsible for my being in this godforsaken place – I adored him.

"We don't share the same blood, it's true, but he's as much my brother as if we'd occupied the same womb for nine months."

"I understand you," Carol gave me a friendly smile. "I feel the same way about Vance; even though we don't have the same mother, he's as much my brother as Josh is."

I felt a pang of sympathy for the red-haired teenager, but I quickly suppressed it. I didn't intend to spend any more time on this ranch than I had to, and the last thing in my plans was to get attached to its inhabitants.

2

Carol escorted me to my room, a spacious bedroom furnished simply but tastefully. A French door opened onto a balcony with a continuous railing that ran from one end of the facade to the other, offering a breathtaking view of the rugged range of snow-capped peaks. After poking around for a while, I unpacked the meager luggage I had brought with me and collapsed onto the double bed, covered with a gorgeous blanket of some wretched animal skin.

"Whoa, what a hut!," I murmured, tangling my fingers in the soft, warm fur.

Drowsily, I decided to take a nap until dinnertime, and as soon as I finished setting the alarm on my phone, I fell asleep.

The alarm ripped me out of a deep sleep two hours later. I awoke with a huge yawn and made my way to the incredible marble bathroom, which was a shocking contrast to the one in the dingy apartment I had lived in for the past few years.

Raff had been very angry when he had visited me in that miserable apartment, but I had weathered the downpour without flinching. My brother knew for a fact that I had never – except for the occasional loan, which I had repaid at the first opportunity – ever taken his money, and I never would. I was too independent, or maybe too proud. Actually, I didn't care in the least what the real reason was. I felt that both Raff and his mother had already done too much for me. So from the time I turned sixteen, I had worked at whatever came up to pay my expenses. Later, when I was offered a scholarship to study at one of the most prestigious dance schools in the country, I was forced to accept Raff's financial help for a few years to support myself and pay for the room in the apartment I shared with two other classmates. As soon as I could, however, I repaid him every cent, despite his protests. Just because my brother was a multimillionaire didn't mean I couldn't take care of myself. That was one of my rules, as I kept telling him. And even though things had gotten pretty bleak lately, I had stubbornly stuck to that maxim.

I washed my face and pulled my hair back in a hurry, without even looking at myself in the mirror. For some time now, I had shied away from the image of that skeletal, grim-faced stranger in my reflection. Without bothering to change out of the wrinkled clothes I had worn all day for something more presentable, I descended the wooden stairs in search of the dining room. As I hesitated in the foyer, wondering which way to go, the front door burst open and a massive figure stepped through, accompanied by a gust of icy wind and a myriad of snowflakes. Both his sheepskin-lined jacket and the Stetson hat that obscured most of his face were covered in frost, and the newcomer was forced to lean his full weight against the door to close it. Once he had achieved his goal, he shook his heavy boots hard on the matting before bending down to untie the laces.

"I love the weather in Wyoming!" I exclaimed in mock delight.

The man looked up from his boots for a few seconds and looked at me in surprise. "Aisha Brooks?" he finally asked in a deep voice that seemed to come from deep inside his chest.

"The one and only."

The shadow of the brim of his hat still hid the man's face, so I had no way of guessing the look on his face when he heard my impertinent reply. Without saying a word, he turned his full attention back to the laces of his boots until he managed to untie them and take them off. After leaving them at the side of the door, he stood up to his full height, which, despite being barefoot, was more than considerable.

"It's difficult to untie shoelaces with half-frozen fingers," he said gently. "Welcome to the Double B, Aisha Brooks. I'm Vance." He held out his hand for me to shake, and it was indeed icy cold.

After the introductions were made, he quickly took off his jacket and hung it on one of the wooden hangers nailed to the wall. Then he shook the hat a few times against his thigh and placed it on another. When he was done, he turned to me, his fingers still running through his flattened hair. It was the first time I could see his features clearly.

"You look nothing like your brother," I blurted out.

His green eyes narrowed slightly as if he had just smiled, though his mouth remained serious. "No? Wow, you break my heart. I hear Josh's quite the ladies' man."

Yes, Josh was a very handsome young man, but the same could not be said for the man in front of me. Vance Bennet wasn't a young man to begin with, but a man in his prime, and he certainly couldn't be described as handsome. His features were too jagged to merit the label. High cheekbones, an aquiline nose, an aggressively square jaw, and dark brown hair, though he wore it short, gave him the appearance of a somewhat wild Apache chief. Only his eyes, an indefinable green that changed with the light, were out of tune with the rest of the ensemble and stood out incongruously in the swarthy face.

"Do you have Indian blood?" My tactlessness didn't seem to bother him in the least.

"I'm thirty percent Sioux, ten percent Mexican, twenty percent German, and forty percent Scottish." Again, the corners of his eyes crinkled almost imperceptibly. "My father always said I was an unpredictable fellow. According to him, it was impossible to know which race would take the lead in my brain and heart at any given moment."

"Fascinating." I pretended to stifle a yawn, but apparently – as I had already ascertained with the younger brother – the Bennets were not the type to be easily offended. The only reaction from the gigantic individual in front of me was to narrow his eyes a little more, with that peculiar silent chuckle.

That was when Tessa appeared. She had changed for dinner and was wearing a very elegant dress.

"So you've met…" Her suspicious eyes darted from one to the other.

"Yes, your *son*," I emphasized the word mockingly, "has already filled me in on how much more complicated his life will be the day he needs a blood transfusion."

Tessa frowned in confusion, but Vance just laughed and, holding our elbows, took his place between us and led us into the dining room, chatting about the weather forecast.

Josh and Carol were already sitting at the table.

"Aren't you going to use the pasture behind the equipment shed this year?" Josh asked with a mouthful of bread, earning a disapproving look from his mother.

"You could at least wait for us to sit down, Josh."

"Sorry, Mom, I'm starving."

"I'll wait another year," his brother replied, "after the coccidiosis outbreak two years ago, I'd rather not risk it. You know, the wet muddy ground is a great breeding ground when the bacteria are still dormant. By the way, Miguel says that this year we have almost twice as many pregnant cows as last year. The new bull is well worth what we paid for him."

"Do we really need to discuss these things at the dinner table?" Tessa protested in a soft voice. "I remind you that we have a guest."

"Don't worry about me, Tessa, I don't mind at all." I smiled a sweet smile that made me look like naivety personified. "This talk of pregnancy and bulls is so... erotic. I've met so many guys in my life who brag about being macho and then don't measure up, I can't wait to meet the real thing." Carol, who had just taken a sip of water from her glass, choked and began to cough and, seeing Tessa's shocked expression, the two older brothers exchanged a look of amusement.

The entrance of a short, dark-haired woman with Hispanic features, carrying a tray larger than herself, dissipated the slight tension in the atmosphere. The woman placed the tray in front of Vance, who inhaled the smell of the stew with relish before turning to me. "This is Fernanda, the person in charge of feeding the ranch's ever-famished stomachs. Her fame as a cook has long since crossed state lines."

"There's no better beef roast in Wyoming than yours, Fernanda!" Josh shouted from across the table.

"You Bennett brothers are quite the flatterers, aren't you?" The woman shook her head in mock disapproval, though it was obvious she was pleased by the compliments.

"Pass me your plate, Aisha, you're going to taste the magnificent meat we produce at the Double B." My host stretched out his hand ready to serve me a good portion.

"Sorry, Vance, I don't eat meat." There was a stony silence, and I said to myself, slightly amused, that if I'd declared myself a nymphomaniac and a serial killer to boot, I wouldn't have caused a bigger stir.

"You don't eat meat?" More than a question, it was an accusation delivered in five different voices.

"No, I'm sorry." It wasn't true at all, but I was determined to be as annoying as possible, so I made a rueful face, "just thinking about those poor defenseless little cows…"

"*¡Menuda pendejada!*" Fernanda muttered in Spanish and I had to bite my lip hard to hide a smile.

"And what are you going to eat?" Josh looked at me with the same pity as if I had just announced I had three days to live.

"Tofu salad, or if not, a glass of almond milk with whole grain crackers. Whatever's out there, I'll settle for anything."

"Almond milk? On a cattle ranch?" Fernanda's dark eyes brimmed with contempt; it was clear that I was beginning to get on her nerves in my role as a chirpy guest.

"Soy, then." I smiled with exquisite friendliness.

As the woman's cheeks began to turn a dangerous shade of purple, Vance, who hadn't taken his eyes off me during the entire exchange, intervened with an inscrutable expression, "I'm sure Fernanda prepared some vegetables to go with the meat, didn't you?" He shot a warning look at the cook, who pursed her lips.

"I'll get the garnish," she finally said, slamming the door as she left the dining room.

"You're not mad, are you?" I opened my eyes wide. "I hope I'm not being a nuisance."

Tessa opened her mouth to speak, but her stepson was quicker. "Of course not, we're very tolerant of other people's ways on this ranch, aren't we?" The way he raised his eyebrows was very eloquent, and the others nodded docilely.

At that moment, Fernanda returned with a bowl of broccoli, which she placed next to my arm with a thud. Undeterred, I gave her an angelic smile, which elicited another snort.

"I heard Jeff Johnson dropped out of college and is going back to his parents' ranch," Carol interjected diplomatically.

The timely change of subject allowed the rest of the dinner to pass without incident. I barely paid attention to the conversation, too focused on my leg, which was starting to hurt again, and planning my immediate future. Still pushing the broccoli from one side of the plate to the other with my fork – for months now, and this was true, I had completely lost my appetite – I decided that I would continue in this vein until I was asked to leave. Raff, who knew me too well, had made me promise that I would stay there for as many months as the judge deemed necessary; but if they were the ones who threw me out, I would not break my promise, I told myself, trying to appease a guilty conscience.

I looked up from my plate and my eyes met Vance's as he studied me intently. For a few moments, I was unable to look away, and I had the strange feeling that those piercing, color-shifting eyes could read my mind without the slightest difficulty. Feeling uncomfortable, I suppressed the impulse to stir in my chair.

"Aren't you eating?" His deep voice startled me.

"I'm not hungry. I'm really very tired." This time I wasn't lying, I was struggling to keep my eyes open and the pain in my leg was becoming unbearable.

"I understand. I wanted to talk to you tonight, but I think it would be better to wait until tomorrow."

Fernanda's appearance with a bowl of rice pudding interrupted us. "I made Josh's favorite dessert, I hope you'll be able to eat it." Her tone was sarcastic.

I placed my palms on the table and stood up. "I'm not hungry, thank you. If you don't mind, I'm going to bed. It's been a long day."

Without waiting for an answer, I quickly left the dining room, forcing myself to limp as little as possible. I was sure that within a few seconds the comments of the other diners would begin to bubble up like water in a boiling cauldron, and I was not wrong. Curious, I put my ear to the door, which I had left ajar on my way out.

"It's hard to believe that a man as charming as Raff could have such a rude girl for a sister! Of course, they're not even siblings." Tessa's malicious tone made me angry. How true it was that eavesdroppers never hear any good of themselves.

"She doesn't eat meat, she doesn't eat rice pudding...!" Fernanda's indignant tones could be heard above the rest. "Apparently, the *señoritinga* doesn't eat broccoli either!"

Vance's unmistakable voice reprimanded them both without losing his composure. "Tessa, Aisha better not hear you making comments like that; I understand that Raff and she have a very close relationship. And you, Fernanda, try to be understanding. Miss Brooks has just arrived in a strange place where she will be forced to spend several months against her will. Under the circumstances, it is normal for her to be a little... tense."

"Tense!" Now it was his brother who spoke, and I suspect he did so with a mouthful of rice pudding. "Say rather a real pisser. She hasn't stopped cutting me since I picked her up at the airport."

Carol stepped in at that moment, "Well, I liked her. It's true she was unfriendly and rude, but I like her eyes."

"You like her eyes?"

"Don't laugh, Vance, haven't you noticed? When she's not lost in unpleasant thoughts, they sparkle with amusement."

I heard the noise they made with the chairs when they got up, and I hurried up the stairs so they wouldn't catch me peeping.

3

When I went downstairs for breakfast the next morning, the dining room was deserted, and I found no one in the living room. Curious, I explored further and came upon a spacious kitchen. There was Fernanda, sitting at a huge pine table, deep in concentration, plucking a chicken and humming a *ranchera*.

"What, murdering helpless animals since early in the morning?"

The woman raised her head in surprise and frowned when she saw me leaning against the door frame with my arms crossed over my chest in a clearly defiant attitude. "About time you got up, *señoritinga*, they all left a while ago."

I shrugged, unimpressed by the unfriendly tone. "Why should I get up early? I have nothing to do."

Fernanda pursed her lips in disapproval and replied, "There are a thousand things to do on a ranch. For now, you can help me take the feathers off these chickens."

"What's it? Didn't the tequilas at breakfast agree with you? I don't touch that stuff, it's disgusting." I walked over to the huge Aga stove and lifted the lids of several bubbling pots to peek inside. "No coffee? What do you have for breakfast? Chicken blood?"

"Yes, of course," this time Fernanda's voice oozed sarcasm. Despite her small size, it was obvious that the cook was not the type to be pushed around, "we mix it with the tequila so it's more nutritious."

In spite of myself, I was forced to suppress a smile.

"Sit down," she said.

She got up to get the carafe from the electric coffeepot on one of the countertops. This time I decided it would be wiser to obey; I needed a good dose of coffee in my veins in the morning to get me going.

"Here." She placed a mug with the Double B branding iron screen-printed on the porcelain and a plate full of small homemade doughnuts in front of me.

"Thanks, but I only drink coffee at this time of day."

"Well, you'll have some doughnuts this morning." I frowned and looked at her with resentment; this woman sure liked to boss around. "You're going to have to be strong to help me."

"Help you?" I raised an arrogant eyebrow. "I remind you that I'm a guest in this house."

Fernanda poured the coffee into the mug, added two spoonfuls of sugar and a good splash of milk.

"Hey, what are you doing, you might ask!" I gave her one of my best dirty looks.

"You're all bones and skin, you won't attract a man looking like that," said the witch, and sat down again to pluck the chickens.

"And who told you that I'm interested in attracting a man, little wetback?"

"I'm not a wetback, I'm an American citizen. I was born here fifty-five years ago."

"Make that seventy-six."

"Once you put on a little weight," she continued as if she hadn't heard me, "we'll have to do something about your filthy tongue. Maybe something drastic..."

With the pad of her thumb, she stroked the edge of the huge knife she held at her side, and once again I had to press my lips together to keep from smiling. I stirred the coffee with a grim expression on my face and after taking a good sip, I grimaced at the sweet taste, "Disgusting."

However, the latte went down better in my stomach than the loaded mixture I usually made. I glanced sideways at the woman who was concentrating on plucking the second chicken before I reached out, grabbed one of the doughnuts from the plate, and took a bite. The tender dough melted in my mouth with a surprising explosion of spicy flavors – cinnamon, ginger, and a few others I didn't recognize – and I closed my eyes to savor the pleasure without distraction. When I opened them again, I found dark, mischievous eyes staring back at me.

"Not bad." I continued to chew with an indifferent expression.

"As Vance said, my fame as a cook extends beyond the borders of the state," she said without the slightest modesty. "What's that? Are you sick?"

I had just taken some pills out of my pocket, which I swallowed with the help of the coffee.

"Are you always so nosy?" I hated being the target of people's curiosity. "It's clear that I'm going to be the talk of the town in this godforsaken place."

Fernanda let out one of her characteristic snorts; she must have picked it up from the cows or the horses. "Don't think you're so fascinating, *señoritinga*, a sack of bones like you isn't interesting enough for half an episode of a soap opera."

I took another angry bite of the doughnut. What did this woman know about whether my life was good enough for a soap opera full of tearful drama or not? Ignoring me, Fernanda continued her work without stopping her humming. Her expression of concentration didn't change when she saw me take the second roll, but I'm sure she was mentally congratulating herself: not even that faded little bitch, who looked as if she hadn't eaten a bite in months, could resist her pastries.

As soon as I finished the second doughnut and drank the rest of the coffee, Fernanda got up and, without saying a word, put a pile of potatoes and a sharp knife in front of me.

"You're crazy if you think..."

"Peel and shut up!"

For the next two hours I peeled one potato after another from that huge pile that seemed to have no end, while this insufferable woman busied herself with the oven and the pans. It would have been a delightful traditional scene depicting daily life if it weren't for the sharp barbs flying back and forth. I didn't hesitate to fire off the first snide remark that came to mind, and the little witch would immediately retaliate with an even sharper one.

So when Vance came into the kitchen in the middle of the morning, he found us most amused in our relentless duel of wits.

"Did you think it was the horses that had horns? I'm sure you'd mistake a cuckoo for a bald eagle as well," Fernanda was saying in a sarcastic tone.

"Of course not! After this pleasant morning together, I'm sure the only cuckold on this ranch is your husband," I blurted out with a look of innocence as angelic as it was false.

"Don't you dare talk like that about my Miguel!"

"Ahem," Vance cleared his throat a few times. "I'm glad you're getting to know each other."

The horsewoman snorted contemptuously, but her boss remained calm, as if he hadn't noticed the hostile atmosphere in the kitchen.

"I can tell you've had a good time with Fernanda." Vance's eyes fell on my face in approval. "Your cheeks are slightly rosy and you look much more cheerful."

"Is it lunch already?" Fernanda shot an alarmed glance at the big wall clock.

"No, don't worry. We just finished feeding the cattle and I thought it would be a good time to have a chat with my guest. Are you coming, Aisha?"

I stood up and gave the cook a triumphant look.

"That busybody had me peeling potatoes all morning. Something that, to be honest, doesn't say much for the Double B's hospitality."

"You don't say," Vance said politely, holding the door open for me.

"I think *you should fire her*," I emphasized the words in a slightly louder tone so that my message would be clearly heard all the way to the kitchen, where it would most likely be greeted with a long-suffering look to the heavens.

"I take note." My host closed the office door.

I looked around curiously. As in the rest of the ranch, the warmth of wood dominated the decor. A floor-to-ceiling bookcase occupied one wall, but as far as I could tell, the books were mostly old farm almanacs and thick, soporific-looking manuals on ranching.

"I can see you're not into romance." Since the accident, sarcasm had become as essential to my existence as the air I breathed.

"Maybe I don't read many romances, but I assure you I'm a romantic guy."

He pointed to one of the chairs in front of an antique desk, and I dropped into it none too gently.

He walked around the table and sat down across from me. We stared at each other in silence for a few seconds, and I was forced to correct my first impression of Vance Bennet. It was true that his features were jagged, but overall his tough-guy appearance was not unattractive. That morning, he was wearing a maroon plaid flannel shirt that accentuated the tan of his skin and the width of his shoulders. You could tell he was a man accustomed to the outdoors, and he already had some fine lines at the corners of his eyes. I couldn't help but compare him to Eric, whose pale body, both sinewy and delicate, I had so often caressed. Nor did the short dark hair have anything to do with the long blond waves of my ex-boyfriend. In fact, I couldn't imagine two men more different.

"Does your leg hurt?" He asked solicitously.

Annoyed at myself for wasting my time with stupid comparisons, I raised my chin in a defiant gesture. "Why would it hurt?"

"Your expression suddenly clouded." The man was too perceptive for my taste, and he looked like he was going to be as nosy as his cook, if not more so. "Raff tells me you're still in pain, even though it has been several years since the accident."

"Don't pay too much attention to Raff. My brother still sees me as a helpless child in need of protection. It's because of his overdeveloped protective instinct that I'm forced to be here."

My host, his elbows resting on the arms of the chair and rhythmically smacking his lips with his index fingers, never took his eyes off my face. I had the impression that he took a few seconds too long to answer.

"I thought," he said finally, "that your stay here was the sentence the judge gave you for your suicide attempt."

Too bad the looks couldn't kill, or I would have put him down right then and there.

"I'm tired of repeating the same thing over and over again!" I raised my voice in anger. "First my brother, then the judge, and now you. How many times do I have to say it? I didn't try to kill myself!"

Without losing his composure, Vance raised both hands in the air, and that simple gesture was far more effective than yelling at me to shut up. I pressed my lips together tightly, even though I wanted to scream some more.

"A codeine overdose isn't a suicide attempt?"

Again, I had to make a superhuman effort to force myself to speak calmly, "It's true that after the accident I ended up hooked on Vicodin, a painkiller I was prescribed. That's the risk you sometimes take with opiates," I shrugged, "but Raff forced me to go through detox for over a year, and I stopped. I'm not even on methadone or antidepressants anymore."

The piercing green eyes wouldn't leave my face, and I doubted very much that anyone could lie under the weight of such a gaze. But I didn't have to explain myself to him either, so I remained silent, challenging him with my own.

"And?" He asked in the same calmed tone he had used throughout the conversation and, I don't know why, I suddenly felt compelled to justify myself.

Without looking up from my hands clasped in my lap, I began to speak in a flat monotone, "I hadn't taken anything stronger than Advil in a long time. I had had a very difficult day." I forced myself not to think about Eric's betrayal. I knew that if I did, I would fall apart and I would never forgive myself if I shed a single tear in the presence of that cowboy, as expressionless as an Indian totem pole. "My leg was killing me and I told myself that for this once, nothing would happen."

I noticed my hands trembling and hid them between my thighs.

"I took a much smaller amount than I was used to, telling myself I was in no danger, but…" I was silent again, shaken.

I could not remember that day without thinking of what had been about to happen. I lifted my eyes to look at him before continuing, "If a gossipy neighbor, whom Raff had bribed to keep him informed of my movements, hadn't called him, I would have died." I made no effort to hide the truth. "I had the immense good fortune that Raff was at a meeting in Los Angeles that very day. I'm afraid that was one of the few deals he didn't close because of me; he stood up a bunch of CEOs of some very important companies and came to the rescue. He even told me that he had to break down the door like in the movies."

There was no trace of amusement in my smile.

"The doctor who treated me was the one who explained to me that if you start using again, there is a great risk of overdose. Apparently, abstinence reduces tolerance to the drug, and even with a much smaller amount, you can easily kick the bucket."

Again there was silence and this time it was he who broke it, "I am glad to know that you are not a frustrated suicide, Aisha, I despise cowards. I see Raff didn't fool me when he told me you were a fighter."

I shrugged when I heard that. "I never understood why suicides are called cowards. Just thinking about how I almost died that day still makes me shudder."

"Good." Vance tapped his fingertips on the desk a few times. "Now that I've ruled out the possibility of you committing suicide on my ranch, with all the paperwork that would entail, I want to make a few things clear."

His cold, determined tone made me frown, but I waited for him to continue. "There's a lot of work to be done on a ranch, so I expect you to get up early and do your part."

I couldn't believe my ears.

"No way! You said yourself, I'm a guest. Besides, my leg hurts, I can't do any physical work."

"This accident might have ended your career as a ballet star." The cruelty of this unnecessary reminder made me look at him with hatred, but he continued undaunted, "But life goes on. You can be as nasty as you want, but you heard the judge: you'll be staying at the Double B for the next months, or you'll be locked up in a state mental institution for attempted suicide."

"I already told you...!"

"Save the shouting, Aisha." The coolness with which the man spoke was getting on my nerves. "You know how the law works in the state of California. You are lucky your brother was able to convince the judge to go with this solution. From what Raff told me, it wasn't easy."

Although I was shaking with anger, I was not stupid. I knew for a fact that only my brother's powerful powers of persuasion and his successful track record as a businessman had kept me from spending a long time in a mental institution. So, despite having to exercise superhuman restraint for the umpteenth time, I managed to ask in a tense but calm voice, "And my leg?"

Vance pulled some papers out of the small pile of documents on one side of the table and flipped through them for a few moments. "This is a report from your doctor."

"You talked to my doctor?!" The volume of my voice shot up again, uncontrollably.

"A very nice man, Dr. Collins," he nodded nonchalantly.

"I'll report him!" I spat through my clenched teeth.

"It's not worth it, Aisha. As you will see, I am a man used to getting what I want." Though his expression was still friendly, I could not miss the veiled warning in his words. "Dr. Collins says you can start training now. He even adds that if you take it easy, the very routines of your ballerina training could be beneficial in regaining almost full mobility."

"Nothing I do can bring back what I've lost!" My voice dripped with bitterness. Endless self-pity gushed from every pore of my skin with the force of a spring.

He didn't look particularly moved. "Maybe not, but he's one of the best in his field, and he believes that the more you move, the less pain you'll have. There's a room with an exercise bike next to yours. No one will bother you there. By the way," he changed the subject without waiting for my answer, "Josh tells me your clothes aren't appropriate for the Wyoming winter, so we're going shopping this afternoon."

His cordial tone did not fool me. I could tell that the owner of the Double B expected his orders to be carried out to the letter, and that certainty pissed me off. I stood up, placed my palms on the leather surface of the desk, and brought my face close to his until the tips of our noses were less than ten inches apart.

"The Great Chief has spoken. Surely you expect me to respond, Hau, don't you?" I challenged him with a sneer. "Just so you know, I'll never take orders from a hick like you."

My aggressiveness did not provoke the slightest reaction from him, and he remained impassive throughout my furious tirade, never taking his eyes off my face. We stayed like this for a few minutes, challenging each other with our gazes, and I had to resist the almost unbearable urge to be the first to look away. There was an unyielding force in that gaze, now more golden than green, that I had never seen before except in my brother Raff's eyes – though never directed at me – that made my heart beat faster.

Vance rose slowly, his palms also resting on the leather surface, and moved closer until his lips almost brushed my ear. This unexpected reaction made my heart race even faster.

"Hear me well, little city princess." The cold whisper tingling in my ear made me shiver. "Raff is very concerned about you and has given me the green light to use whatever methods I deem appropriate during your stay at my ranch. So don't expect any help on that front. You have two options: stay here and obey my orders, or the mental institution. Your choice."

Fortunately, the door burst open at that moment, saving me from having to give an answer. I took the opportunity to step back and immediately felt a colossal relief as the uncomfortable proximity ceased.

"What's going on here?"

The newcomer stood at the door with her hands on her hips, her eyes darting from him to me and back, full of suspicion.

"Zoe, how many times do I have to tell you to knock before you come in?"

Apparently this guy never lost his cool. Seeing his relaxed attitude, this Zoe girl also relaxed a bit, although when she turned to me, she swept me up and down with a flash of jealousy in her expressive honey-colored eyes.

Jealousy!, I said to myself, amused. Was it possible that someone who saw me as I was now could be jealous of me? Suddenly I realized that this was a good opportunity to annoy the insufferable Vance Bennet, and I didn't hesitate. I might have no choice but to obey his orders – it was very clear to me that going to the nuthouse was not an option – but at least I would try to make his life miserable during the months I would be forced to spend there.

"Well, Vance, darling, it's been lovely..." I let the sentence hang in the air for a second and ran my tongue over my upper lip, "chatting with you. You're such a considerate and thoughtful man and, why not say it, so incredibly attractive that I'll have to be very careful not to fall in love with you."

I let out a flirtatious chuckle, to which he replied with a gentle smile.

"You are very kind, Aisha. By the way, I guess you know that all of us who live and work at the ranch eat together in the bunkhouse behind the house. I hope to see you there for lunch. I would appreciate it if you could help Fernanda. Even though she gets mad if we say anything, she's not so young anymore, and feeding so many mouths is hard work."

"I'm afraid that's going to be difficult, Vance, dear. You know," I shrugged ruefully, "doctor's orders."

Without giving him time to reply, I left the office, closing the door gently and, of course, I stood listening on the other side.

"And who's that?" There was a universe of jealousy in that simple question.

"This is Aisha Brooks, my friend Raff's sister. I told you she would be spending some time with us."

"There's something murky about her. I don't know…, I just don't trust her. How long is she gonna stay?"

"As long as it takes."

I imagined her pursing her lips in disgust.

"I just hope you're nice to her, Zoe. Aisha Brooks is not having the time of her life." I pressed my lips together; if there was one thing I hated in the world, it was being pitied. "Anyway, I have to go check on the hands. I'll see you later."

I hurried away from the door and managed to duck around a bend in the hallway before he caught me in the act. I heard Vance wave to someone passing by and then the office door opened again.

"Hi, little Zoe. How's it going?" an unfamiliar male voice asked.

The year I had spent working at the Nolan Detective Agency had taught me that information was power. So I tiptoed over and put my ear to the door again, determined to eavesdrop some more.

"Good God! More boring stuff?" There was a note of resentment in Zoe's voice.

"You know there's a lot of paperwork this time of year."

"I'm sick of it! It's not fair that I have to be cooped up in this boring office all day while you guys do the cool work." She spoke with the whine of a spoiled little girl, and I couldn't resist the urge to mock her from behind the door.

"Talk to Vance."

"I told him a thousand times! It's Josh who's supposed to be here, that's why he's taking this correspondence course in business administration, right? I only have a lousy accounting degree."

"Don't get mad at me, Zoey. It's worse to be a distant relative employed at the ranch almost for charity than it is to be the daughter of Vance's father's best friend."

"Don't call me Zoey! It's a horrible pet name!"

The man burst out laughing, then spoke again, "You looked at me for a long time and sighed, does that mean you're finally falling in love with me?"

The guy was a tireless flirt.

"No way. Like most cowboys, you're a loner, and like the rest of them, you don't like to stay in one place for too long. I imagine it's quite a feat for a man like you to have stayed in the Double B for almost two years."

"It's your very presence that binds me to this place."

I almost gagged when I heard that tired phrase, but apparently Zoey wasn't a complete idiot.

"Don't even try, Colin, I know for a fact that you fool around with all the women. I'll never be one of those dumb girls who fall for your charm."

"I'm afraid the boss got here before me, didn't he?"

"Go away, don't distract me anymore, I've got a lot to do." Judging by the dryness of Zoe's tone, that had stung.

Again I had to run to avoid being discovered. Safe in my hiding place in the hallway, I smiled, satisfied with my detective work. At least I knew a little more about the inhabitants of this ranch, and as my old boss always said: "Information is power, and power is the spice of life."

4

At one o'clock sharp, the metallic sound of a bell rang through my bedroom door, where I had taken refuge to escape Fernanda's clutches. For a few moments I thought about ignoring it, but to my surprise I realized that even though I had eaten much more than usual at breakfast, I was hungry. So I went down to the kitchen.

One of the doors in the large kitchen led to the bunkhouse, so there was no need to go outside and suffer the inclement weather. I was infinitely glad of that when I heard the threatening howl of the wind and the force with which the hail struck the window panes.

"Pick up that pot of meat and bring it over here. Quickly!"

I raised my eyes to the sky, tempted to let that employee, who carried herself with the air of a great duchess, know how little her orders meant to me, but when I saw her disappear into the next building without looking back, I shook my head in disgust and, after putting on a pair of kitchen gloves that I had also found on the table, I grabbed the handles of the heavy pot. With a grunt, I picked it up and followed her.

As soon as I entered, a blast of hot air hit me, mixed with the smell of wet wool and sweat, and I had the feeling that the bunkhouse was full of men talking loudly. A rustic wooden table ran almost from one end of the room to the other, and the cowboys, all wearing their hats, occupied the benches placed along the length of the table, chatting and laughing. I didn't have time to observe more details, because the pot was heavy as hell. Panting, I narrowly avoided hitting the man at the head of the table with it and placed it on the table without too much delicacy.

"Surprising. You're much stronger than you look."

I instantly turned my head to find Vance looking at me with one of his vile, unsmiling smiles. "If I get a muscle cramp from this kind of forced labor, I'll report you to the authorities," I replied grumpily.

"Enough chitchat, *señoritinga*, and start serving!" Fernanda shouted from the other end of the table as she filled the plates of the men closest to her to the brim.

"Hey, it's okay. I'll help you." Vance's hand came to rest on mine, which in an unconscious gesture had closed tightly around the handle of the ladle, and he gently made me to drop the contents of the ladle onto his plate.

"You'll have to tell that old hag that I'm not her slave." I didn't bother to lower my voice and immediately there was silence and everyone in the room turned to look at me.

With his fingers still wrapped around my wrist, despite my efforts to free myself, Vance took the floor. "Boys, this is Aisha Brooks. Aisha will be here for the next few months. As you can see, she's a city girl, so I'm sure she'll love hearing all about cattle and ranch life.

"Stick with me, blondie, I'm the voice of experience!" shouted a gray-haired cowboy. "Ain't that right, boss?

The room was filled with laughter and teasing remarks, and Vance, who listened to the more or less off-color jokes with a faint smile on his lips, pretended not to see the hostile look I gave him, though I'm sure he was well aware of it. Finally, he let go of me and raised his hand to ask for silence. "Anyway, boys, don't scare her too much. Aisha is a shy girl."

I faced him angrily, but this time I was careful to speak softly. "I don't like your little jokes."

"Aren't you shy? You've turned red."

"It's probably anger, because I'm not shy at all."

"I apologize." Vance, who had been filling the dishes as he spoke, pointed to the empty chair to his left. "Come sit over here and eat before it gets cold."

I noticed that several of the hands were looking at me sideways, so I decided not to make a scene and reluctantly obeyed. The delicious smell of the beef stew made my bad mood disappear and I began to eat with an appetite. The man next to me watched me out of the corner of his eye with a smug expression that I didn't like at all.

"Did you notice," he pointed to the last piece of meat on my plate, "that this is not tofu?"

I pierced the meat with my fork and raised it to my mouth in clear defiance.

"I decided to adapt to the circumstances, even against my principles." I gave him an angelic smile. "I don't want you to think I'm an inconvenient visitor."

"Of course not, Aisha. It is a pleasure to have you with us."

I couldn't detect a trace of irony in his tone. Annoyed, I decided to concentrate on the generous slice of cheesecake someone had just placed in front of me. But after a few bites, I couldn't eat any more and pushed it aside.

"May I?" Without waiting for an answer, Vance took my plate and finished the rest of the cake.

Then, as if someone had given the signal, the cowboys stood up, walked over to the coat racks to get their jackets, and soon the bunkhouse was empty except for Fernanda, her boss, and me. Vance finished buttoning his sheepskin-lined jacket, pulled his Stetson down to his eyebrows, and turned to me. "Today's your first day, so get some rest. I'll pick you up in a few hours to go shopping."

Before I had time to protest, he opened the door and disappeared into one of those unpleasant swirling blizzards.

"*La señoritinga* needs to rest, she has worked so hard..." The cook's sarcastic remark made me turn my head, a dangerous glint in my eyes.

"You heard the boss, *cholita*. While you pick this up," I pointed to the table full of dirty plates and glasses, "I'm going to lie down for a while in my wonderful bed, well wrapped in my no less wonderful fur blanket."

Fernanda shook her head with tight lips. "*Muchacha del diablo*, you're going to learn a lesson you won't forget," she muttered, though I understood her perfectly.

I gave her a mocking bow before turning and walking out the door.

I must have been more tired than I thought, because I didn't stir until Vance came to get me.

"Coming! Just a second!"

What a way to bang on the door. Stunned by the rude awakening, I went into the bathroom and quickly washed my face and teeth before opening the door.

"I see you overslept." He ran the back of one of his long brown fingers along the mark on my cheek.

I threw my head back. "I don't like being touched."

"No? Too bad, I'm a very affectionate man." He frowned at my clothes. "You can't wear that jacket, it's too thin. Wait a moment."

He disappeared into the next room and returned with a shearling coat. "It was my father's. He gave it to me when I was a teenager, and even though it no longer fits me, I still keep it."

I declined his help and quickly took off my jacket and put on his oversized coat. Luckily, I remembered to throw a wooly hat and gloves in my pocket.

Once we were in the foyer, the guy with the daddy complex made me stop in front of him. Ignoring my protests, he began rolling up one sleeve and then the other to free my hands before buttoning my coat up to my chin.

"You look like a malnourished orphan."

I detected a trace of… tenderness? in his voice, but I chose to take offense. "I can't stand being treated like a little girl."

"I'll have to make a list of everything you can't stand, my memory isn't as good as it used to be."

The cowboy's good humor was incombustible and I wanted to scream. I noticed that he frowned as he looked at my feet. "Your boots are beyond useless and Carol's are at least four sizes too big. Anyway, we'll take care of it soon."

"Are we going to Jackson?"

"No, we're going to Wilson. It's closer and there's a little store that sells what you need. Put on your hat and gloves."

I pulled my woolen hat down to my eyebrows without the slightest coquetry, and again I detected the same silent smile, though not a muscle had moved on the man's face.

"What is it?" I raised my chin in defiance.

Without answering, Vance pulled on his own hat, opened the front door, and motioned for me to come out. As soon as he closed it, strong fingers wrapped around my arm to lead me to the truck, and I had no choice but to put up with it. The strong gusts of wind and the thin soles of my boots kept me slipping, and the last thing I wanted was to fall flat on my face on the frozen ground.

Vance held the passenger door open for me and shut it firmly before turning around and climbing in as well.

"Well, I hope you enjoy your afternoon shopping." He started up and turned the heating knob to maximum.

Still, I was glad to be wearing his coat. It was very warm and comfortable and smelled slightly of him.

"Fernanda says you're a very busy man. I don't understand why you're wasting a whole afternoon shopping with me."

"It's a pleasure to be in your company, Aisha."

I rolled my eyes, and although the difficult weather conditions had Vance paying close attention to the road, my gesture was not lost on him.

"You don't believe it?"

"Let's just say that at no time have I ever aspired to be the most popular girl in the Double B," I said, my eyes lost in the blurry gray landscape.

"No, you haven't," he smiled, changing the subject. "Did you know that we've met before?"

I frowned at him, "I think you're wrong." Whatever he was, Vance Bennet was not a man to be easily forgotten.

"It was about six years ago. I was in Los Angeles on business and Raff was there for the same reason. I wanted to meet him for dinner, but Raff said he had two tickets to the ballet. The ballet? I must have made a startled face, because he laughed and commented on how ridiculous he felt the first time he accompanied your mother to one of your performances."

"My mother..." When I heard that, a deep longing came over me. In fact, Raff's mother had been my mother for over fourteen years. I never knew my biological mother, but I don't think she could have been any better than this big, loving woman who made a place in her heart for me when no one else wanted me.

"As you can imagine," Vance continued, and I forced myself to pay attention, "this is not your typical Wyoming rancher's agenda. I hesitated for a few seconds, and then Raff commented that it was your first *prima ballerina* performance, so I had no choice but to accept."

"And you hated every second of it, of course. A hick like you going to the ballet, what a joke." I pouted scornfully.

I had hoped to offend him with this rude remark, but once again I miscalculated. It was clear that the men of the Bennet family were not very touchy.

"You'd think so, wouldn't you? The funny thing is, I loved the show from start to finish. It was *Sleeping Beauty*, and I told myself I'd never seen anything more beautiful than Aurora and the Prince's *grand pas de deux*," he smiled at those memories.

I bit my lips hard. I would never forget that day, one of the happiest days of my life. Not only because my dream of being a *prima ballerina* in one of America's great ballets had finally come true, but because I had danced with Eric, and our movements had flowed like a dream throughout the entire performance. I felt a lump in my throat, and I had to swallow it to keep my voice from shaking.

"Certain things will never cease to amaze me." I tried to sound ironic, but my words were tinged with bitterness. "Anyway, it's strange that I don't remember you."

"Whereas I remember every single detail." I turned to look at him in surprise, but Vance's face, his eyes never leaving the road, remained as calm as ever.

"When the show was over, we went to your dressing room. It was full of people. Everyone was talking and laughing loudly. Someone had brought out a huge bottle of champagne and some plastic glasses and toasts were being made. Then Raff spotted you in the middle of a group of dancers and waved you over. As soon as you saw him, you jumped on him, wrapped your legs around his waist and hugged him with all your might. You were still wearing the dress and tiara of sparkling crystals from the last act. When Raff finally set you down, I was ready to greet you and express my admiration, but just then the prince arrived and, after kissing you on the lips, dragged you off in the direction of another group of people."

"Raff apologized for not being able to make the introductions. It was getting late, so we went to dinner, and from then on I looked forward to meeting this young woman who radiated a special energy that illuminated everything in her path."

I blinked several times to keep my eyes from welling up. The sound of his deep voice as he reminisced about those happy times had given me goosebumps.

"I'm afraid you'll never get your wish," I was proud of the coldness with which I spoke, "that person died in a car accident a few years later."

"Are you sure? I think she's out there somewhere, hiding."

"I don't like you psychoanalyzing me."

"I'll add it to my list of taboo subjects."

"You think you're very funny, don't you?"

"Not at all." He shook his head without taking his eyes off the road. "I've always been a serious man, you know. It's my twenty percent German blood."

I let out an unladylike snort. "There you go again. I'm not at all interested in the extent of your miscegenation. Would you mind not talking any more?"

"Not at all," he repeated good-naturedly, "there's nothing like the silence shared by two old friends."

I gave up. The guy was definitely a cross between Mr. Happy and Pollyanna. No matter how unpleasant I became, there was no way to make him mad.

We drove the few remaining miles to Wilson in silence, or near-silence, because Vance, like his brother, had an irritating habit of humming the same song over and over again.

"We're here!"

I wiped the fog from the window with the sleeve of my coat, but I could barely make out the outlines of a few houses on the side of the road.

"It's very small."

"It has less than fifteen hundred inhabitants, but it has the necessary services."

He stopped the truck in front of a wooden building that seemed to barely withstand the wind. Less than a dozen yards separated us from the warehouse, but my toes still froze on the way.

"Hi, Maude," Vance put two fingers to his hat, but didn't take it off. In fact, I'd only seen him without it when he was in the house and not all the time. "How's business?"

"Getting by, Vance Bennet, just getting by."

"Well, you're in luck, we're here to liven things up. We need to do some shopping."

The woman, who must have been closer to eighty than seventy, came out from behind the old-fashioned wooden counter, walking with some difficulty. I was busy tapping my boots on the floor to get the circulation going, but I still noticed the eager curiosity with which she examined me.

"Is she your girlfriend?" This unexpected conclusion made me stop with one foot in the air.

"No way, madam! Thank God, my good taste is not completely dead." Despite my outburst, the kind expression on the old lady's face did not change at all.

"She's a little city princess, Maude," the cowboy interjected with his usual maddening good humor. "She thinks the people in these parts are all hicks."

The woman chuckled happily. "I used to be like that too, you know, Miss..."

"Brooks, Aisha Brooks," Vance hastened to reply when he noticed my hostile attitude.

I was sorry – well, not really – but I wasn't going to bother contributing my share of inconsequential chatter.

"I'll call you Aisha, if you don't mind." I just shrugged; I couldn't care less what the woman called me. "I came to this city over sixty years ago, you know. My parents had separated, and my mother and I went to live with my grandparents. It was a very difficult transition. Leaving New York, leaving school, leaving my lifelong friends... Like you, I thought this was the end of the world and that its inhabitants were all unrefined yokels. I only dreamed of running away and going back to New York."

I was reluctantly curious, but when I saw Vance looking at me with amusement, I tried to hide it and blurted out with impertinence, "Let me guess... you never made it back to New York."

"Oh, yes, I've been there a couple of times on vacation."

I snorted irritably, at this rate the woman would never finish her story. "But you didn't run away, did you?"

"Oh, no. One day I met my Frank at a dance and from then on we were never apart until pneumonia took him from this world two winters ago."

I noticed tears in her eyes and I felt a little uncomfortable. "I'm sorry," I said quietly.

"Oh, don't be sorry, little one." Maude wiped away a tear with the collar of her flannel shirt. "It was a wonderful love story and I wouldn't change a minute of it for the world."

There was an awkward silence, but fortunately the good woman soon recovered. "I'm just telling you to be careful, Aisha. There's something special about Wyoming men." She winked mischievously at Vance. "And enough with the chitchat, what are you looking for?"

"We need some boots, a real hat, a couple of pairs of sturdy jeans, shirts, undershirts, socks, sweaters, and a warm coat."

I turned to him, my hands on my hips. "Why are you speaking for me? Are you my father? I don't like being spoken for."

With an impassive face, Vance pressed the tips of his index finger and thumb together and pretended to make a note in the palm of his hand, a gesture that made me grit my teeth. Meanwhile, Maude had gone to work and soon had a mountain of shirts, jeans and a pair of sturdy boots on the counter. "Try these on."

I was about to refuse when the door opened and a new customer walked in, accompanied by a blast of icy air that reminded me how cold it was out there. With a grunt, I threw a good pile of clothes over my arm, grabbed the boots, and made my way to the small fitting room I'd seen at the back of the store, disappearing behind some peeling wooden swinging doors that mimicked those of a saloon.

"Come out so we can see you!" Vance yelled.

"Don't hold your breath!"

As I tried on outfit after outfit, I strained to hear the conversation between Maude and the bossy cowboy. I was sure they were talking about me, but even though I heard them laughing a lot, I couldn't make out what they were saying. More and more angry, I finished buttoning my blouse, walked out of the dressing room and roughly set the few clothes I had chosen and the boots on the counter. "I'll take these."

I didn't want to buy too much. I barely had a few hundred dollars left over from what I'd saved from working as a Girl Friday at a detective agency. Actually, that name was a little too grand for the obscure office I'd shared with Chuck, my ex-boss, for the past fourteen months.

Vance picked up the clothes I had discarded and placed them on the pile as well. Then he unhooked a stylish beaver-fur cowboy hat from a hanger, placed it on my head, and looked at me intently. "Very pretty. Add this, Maude."

"I don't need that many things!" I angrily took the hat off.

"Of course you do." He spoke as if I was being irrationally stubborn, which made me even madder. "I guess you're not rolling in riches right now. According to Raff, you refused to take the money he offered you, so consider me your banker."

Afraid of losing control and throwing a straight punch to the square jaw of this overbearing man who tossed orders around with such calm, I clenched my fists against my thighs. "If I didn't take Raff's money, I certainly won't take yours."

Maude and the customer who had walked in a little earlier followed our more than tense exchange without hiding their curiosity.

Vance raised his eyes to the sky, as if inviting his main tenant to arm him with patience. "I'm not offering you money. I'm offering you a loan that I will cash in with whatever tasks I ask you to do."

It was clear that his nagging idea of making me work was serious.

"So I'm not a guest anymore?" I pouted before covering my face with the palms of my hands and pretended to blush. "It's not an indecent proposal, is it?"

He smiled. "No indecent proposals here."

I regained my seriousness and replied in an icy voice, "You can save your sympathy and your employment. I am not qualified to work on a ranch, and I have not the slightest interest in learning."

"Perhaps you could help me in the store," Maude interjected, "I've had a lot of work piling up since my husband died."

"No, thank you."

But the good woman did not give up easily. "Let me see... what were you working on before you came here?"

It seemed that it wasn't customary to hide one's curiosity in this part of the world. I was about to open my mouth to tell her that my business was none of hers when that meddlesome cowboy stepped forward again and answered for me, "She was a *prima ballerina* with the Los Angeles Ballet."

"Really?" That simple word was filled with admiration.

This time I spoke, though my eyes were fixed on Vance. "Of course not, what nonsense!" I said, not trying to hide my resentment. "I haven't danced in over three years. My last job consisted of keeping the books for a small detective agency, answering the phone, investigating some pretty lousy cheating stories, several small-time con artists, and finding a couple of crooks who vanished, leaving their wives' bank accounts bone dry."

Maude gaped in amazement. "How interesting. I hope you come back soon. We can have coffee across the street and you can tell me more." As she spoke, she entered the prices into an antediluvian cash register. Suddenly she looked up at me, excited. "You know? Linda, the school principal, was here the other day, and she said they were looking for someone to organize the end-of-year party. I'll talk to her!"

"Don't bother. I have no intention of staying until the end of the school year."

The woman and the cowboy exchanged an eloquent look before she lowered her eyes back to the cash register keys and resumed her task. "I'll tell her anyway."

I rolled my eyes.

"You still need to pick out a coat," Vance said.

"I'm not buying anything else!" The amount on the cash register had already sent a few chills down my spine.

Vance gave me a sympathetic look that made me grind my teeth once more. "You can have mine, I like the way it looks on you."

Without giving me time to reach into my purse for my wallet, he pulled a wad of bills from his back pocket, held together with a silver paper clip, and paid.

"I said I'm not taking your money!"

"Tomorrow you start working for me. You'll help Fernanda in the morning and clean the stables in the afternoon, and you'll pay what you owe me in no time."

I was not completely stupid. I knew I didn't have enough money, and I knew I had to find a job as soon as possible. But the thought of that infuriating man getting away with it put me in a terrible mood.

"All right, I'll work for you!" Swallowing my pride and accepting his offer was one of the hardest things I had ever done in my life.

Maude let out a cackling laugh that she cut short when she noticed the threatening look I shot her. She finished stuffing everything into several paper bags and handed them to Vance.

"I'm afraid the task you've set for yourself is not going to be easy," she said with a knowing smile.

He shrugged and smiled back. "I like a challenge. I can't help it."

"You know, Charles," Maude turned to the middle-aged man who hadn't said a word all this time, "as old as I am, I can't help but be envious of this young lady."

I was disgusted that everyone talked as if I were not there.

"I hate this hick town!" I kicked the floor like an angry child and stormed out of the warehouse.

The cowboy's imposing, bag-laden figure stood silhouetted against the warehouse door for a few seconds. Vance pulled his hat on tightly and walked toward the truck, head down to protect himself from the wind. I waited shivering inside the pickup, snuggled in my thick coat.

"About time," I said grumpily.

The cowboy threw the bags in the back, started the engine, and repositioned most of the vents so that the hot air hit me directly. "You'll warm up in no time."

I decided to punish his tireless kindness with my silence and spent the entire ride back looking out the window. A punishment that, once again, didn't seem to affect the man next to me at all, who continued to drive, humming the pounding melody of the outward journey.

As soon as he stopped the truck under the wooden pergola next to the house, I knelt down on the seat, grabbed the bags from the back, and opened the door. Without saying goodbye or thanking him, I jumped out awkwardly and walked toward the house. I retreated to my room and only came out when Carol told me dinner was ready. I ate in silence, and as soon as I finished, I stood up and said a laconic 'good night' as I left.

"She sure is rude." I heard Tessa say as I left the dining room. So, as usual, I gave in to my masochistic streak and stood behind the door and listened.

Vance came to my defense without losing his cool. "She's had a rough day."

His stepmother snickered. "Of course, shopping is so hard."

"I saw the pile of bags she brought home." For once, Carol seemed to agree with her mother. "I wish Mom would buy so many things for me when we go shopping, and what's the point? She came to dinner wearing the same old wrinkled pants and didn't even bother to put her hair up properly."

"Sometimes things aren't what they seem, Carol," her elder brother said calmly.

I let out a quiet snort. I couldn't say why, but the nicer he was, the more I resented him.

"Why do you say that, Vance?" As usual, Josh spoke with his mouth full, and I imagined he had just scarfed down another of Fernanda's delicious cream-filled puff pastries.

“Aisha Brooks is a very independent person, and this afternoon her pride took a major blow.”

Yuck, how I hated his pity.

There was silence as the others tried to digest this.

“But I don’t think you need to worry.” As soon as I heard Vance’s amused tone, I could almost see the fine lines that had surely formed at the corners of his green eyes. “I’m sure Miss Brooks will be up to her usual naughty tricks by tomorrow.”

5

The alarm on my cell phone woke me up very early and I immediately remembered that it was my first day as a ranch employee. It was going to take me a while to pay off that pesky cowboy, but I was determined to pay him back every penny.

I reluctantly climbed out of the warm bed, and even though the heater was working fine, I got goose bumps.

"I hate the cold, I hate the cold, I hate the cold," I muttered as I rummaged through the bags for something to wear.

I hadn't paid the slightest attention to my purchases the day before. In fact, everything was still there; I hadn't even bothered to hang the clothes in the closet. But as I touched the brand-new jeans, the warm flannel shirts, and the soft wool sweaters, I realized that I had not bought anything new in years, except for the jacket and boots I'd picked up at a thrift store just before coming to Wyoming. Even though it wasn't the style I usually wore in Los Angeles, I had to admit that the clothes were nice.

I took a quick shower and dressed. As I passed the full-length mirror near the closet, I stopped in surprise. The blue-green of the sweater was very flattering, and for once my cheeks didn't have a sickly tint. The pants fit my narrow hips and, despite the fact that I had slimmed down too much lately, at least I no longer looked like a potato sack. The tall, sheepskin-lined boots were deliciously warm and made my legs look longer.

I raised my arms to pull my hair up in my usual unflattering bun, but thought better of it and left it down after a thorough brushing. It wasn't a brutal change, but the loose hair softened my cheekbones, which were too pronounced from the weight loss. With effort, I looked away from my reflection and walked out of the bedroom.

I had one foot on the first step when I remembered Vance's comment about a room with an exercise bike that no one used. I turned back, approached the door to the right of my bedroom, and carefully peeked in.

"Wow!"

The room was a good size, and although the dawn light was still dim from the bare east-facing windows, I had no trouble making out the huge wall-to-wall mirror, a somewhat old-fashioned exercise bike, and, most surprising of all, a height-adjustable ballet barre.

"Damn you, you busybody!" Again I was overcome with anger.

There was no doubt in my mind that this was Vance Bennet's idea; it bore his unmistakable stamp as the king of meddlers. It was obvious that he was playing the amateur psychologist. Although we barely knew each other, I had already come to understand him: he was the kind of man who would resort to any trick – always with a well-meaning air, of course – to get his own way. My brother Raff was also a bit like that, so I had recognized the type at first glance.

I was very angry, but a force greater than myself pushed me forward to the barre. Slowly I slid my palm over the smooth wooden surface and a flood of images entered my mind: a tiny girl in a pink leotard, very focused on her endless routine of *grands battements, frappés, échappés* and *relevés,* with the sound of the piano in the background; later, a slender young woman in a white romantic tutu doing a *grand rond de jambe en l'air;* and finally, a graceful couple, both very blond, smiling into each other's eyes over a similar barre.

I didn't know how long I stayed like that, completely lost in my memories, but when I finally came back to the present, I noticed that my cheeks were soaked. Annoyed with myself, I roughly dried them with the sleeve of my sweater and went back to my room to wash my face with cold water before going downstairs for breakfast.

Vance, Josh and Carol were already devouring scrambled eggs with thick slices of bacon. As soon as I entered the kitchen, there was a deep silence and three pairs of eyes swept me up and down. Annoyed, I noticed that I was blushing.

"Jeez, Aisha, you look beautiful, doesn't she?"

"Josh is right, you do look beautiful." Carol smiled with sincere admiration.

I looked at Vance, silently daring him to comment, but he said nothing.

"Here. Your coffee and some pancakes." Without asking, Fernanda put everything in front of me. "The boss told me you'll be working hard today, so you'll need all your energy."

I had to bite my tongue and remind myself that a job was a job and sometimes in life there was no choice but to grin and bear it. Without saying a word, I sat down and began to eat with an appetite. Suddenly, I looked up and saw curious green eyes staring at me.

"What are you looking at?"

"You, of course."

"Well, don't, I don't..."

"You don't like being looked at," he finished the sentence for me. "I'll add that to the list".

I bit my lower lip in annoyance. I saw his brother hide a smile, but Vance started talking about the tasks they had ahead of them, and the tension dissipated.

"Carol, you will help in corral two until we finish vaccinating the pregnant cows. Josh, take Brad and a couple of other men to fill the feed bunkers with fodder. Then you guys take care of the horses, we need to separate the stallions from the geldings and the mares. Oh, and Josh, check the fence on three; Al says some of the posts need reinforcing."

"Hey, boss!" the two brothers replied in unison before getting up and walking out of the kitchen.

"What about me, *boss*?" I emphasized the noun with my usual sarcasm.

"Fernanda will tell you what to do."

I turned to frown at the cook, who looked like she was about to lick her lips in satisfaction.

My new boss pretended not to notice and stood up. "See you later."

Fernanda and I were left alone, challenging each other with our eyes.

"That's the thing about life," she finally said, with exaggerated kindness, "it's like a Ferris wheel. some days you're up and some days you're down."

"Keep your starving peasant girl folk wisdom to yourself. I'm not the least bit interested."

"Maybe not, but…" she paused dramatically; boy, was she enjoying herself. "You heard the boss: I'm the one who gives the orders."

"I imagine, being the witch that you are, you already have the broom ready, so hand it over and let's be done with it."

"Well, you're wrong. Two girls from Wilson are coming to do the cleaning. You will help me in the kitchen. We have to prepare the steaks, we're having a barbecue today."

"Meat again?" I used a patronizing tone that didn't fit well with my new humble position as a kitchen assistant.

"Obviously you haven't heard of scurvy around here. My teeth are starting to move in my gums."

"Don't worry about it, *señoritinga*." Fernanda gave me a wicked smile. "The meat will be accompanied by green beans, and guess who's going to peel beans for twenty men with good appetites. For now, start filleting this beef tenderloin," she pointed to a piece of meat the size of a diplodocus, "and try not to cut your fingers, this knife is not a toy."

Resisting the urge to stick my tongue out at her, I picked up the heavy knife and examined the gigantic piece not really knowing where to begin. Fernanda rolled her eyes with a theatrical gesture and began to explain the procedure with exaggerated patience, as if I were a complete idiot. Furious, I gripped the knife handle tighter and fantasized about starting to practice on the cook's petite body.

"Did you get it?"

Her question abruptly pulled me out of my murderous reverie. "I think I did."

I began to cut, and had to endure that insufferable woman's watchful gaze until she was sure I would not stain her spotless kitchen with my blood.

The work in the kitchen was hard, but between that and coming up with witty retorts to the little slave driver's verbal attacks, the morning flew by.

"Looks great," Vance said kindly as I rudely set down a plate of juicy, over-the-rim steak and a hearty helping of green beans in front of him.

"I hope you're thinking of giving me a decent paycheck, because putting up with that harpy barking orders left and right all morning is unbearable."

"Don't worry." He pushed back his ever present hat a bit and gave me a smile that made me blink a few times. "I'm a fair boss."

From her post next to the giant grill, Fernanda waved me over to get more plates.

"See what I mean?" I said indignantly, and called out, "Coming!

Despite my protests, I was having a good time. I liked the way the men joked with me, making racy remarks that were never rude, to which I immediately responded with others, sprinkled with a certain acidity that immediately set off an explosion of laughter.

When Fernanda finished serving everyone, she held a full plate in front of me. I looked around and saw to my dismay that the only empty seat was next to Vance.

"Aren't you going to eat it all?" he asked as he watched me cut into the huge steak and set more than half of it aside. "You should, you're too skinny."

I looked up from my plate with an unfriendly expression. "If I need some fatherly advice, I'll ask for it. Until then, I'd appreciate it if you'd leave me alone."

"I see that your mood is not improving as the days go by."

I continued to chew without answering.

"It's funny." Vance picked up the piece of meat I had set aside and put it on his plate. "The more unkind you are to me, the more I'm convinced that sooner or later your charming side will come out."

My only response was an unladylike snort, but he didn't give up and continued smiling, "You see? Such stubbornness must be a consequence of my forty percent Scottish blood."

"Don't start that again!"

"Sorry, I forgot you don't like to talk about my mixed blood."

I gave him a very artificial smile. "Did I tell you how annoying you can be?"

"Funny," he said, without losing his good humor. "People usually think of me as a nice fellow."

"An-noy-ing" I said breaking the word into syllables so there would be no doubt what I thought of him.

He had the nerve to wink at me and continued eating.

Soon after, I put the silverware down on the plate with a sigh. "Do you want more beans? I'm about to explode."

He scowled at me. "Just for today, okay?" He picked up my plate and poured the rest of the beans onto his. I like a woman who eats with an appetite."

"And should I care?"

"Of course you should, you must try to please those around you."

"My particular bête noire is already beckoning me again, so I'm afraid we'll have to leave this fascinating discussion for another time."

After helping Fernanda clean up, I decided to take a nap. I didn't have to report to the stables for a couple of hours, so I took the opportunity to rest and elevate my leg, which was hurting pretty bad.

The stables were a large, well-lit structure with spacious stalls, each with fresh hay beds and automatic water troughs, and a hive of activity. As soon as I entered, I noticed that the temperature was pleasant in contrast to the cold outside. It smelled of horse, straw, leather, and a hundred other things I couldn't put my finger on. I approached the gray-haired cowboy who had made a joking remark in the dining room on the first day.

"Hi, Vance told me to come and help, but I don't know where to start."

The man leaned against the huge bale of hay he was rolling to the back of the facility and wiped his sweaty brow with a sleeve.

"You've come at a good time, child." I grimaced and had to bite my tongue to keep from giving him a snappy comeback. "Spring calving starts in a few days and it's one of the busiest times on the ranch, so we're cleaning up. We need to spread a thick layer of straw in this corner in case we need a dry, warm place for the sick calves. Then we do the same in the corral so the calves aren't born on a pile of snow or mud. The straw also helps keep the mothers' udders clean."

I tapped the ground with the sole of one of my new boots. These topics didn't interest me in the least. All I wanted was for him to give me a job to do and get it over with as quickly as possible, but the man kept talking, oblivious to my growing impatience.

"Problem is, you're a lightweight and you can't handle one of these."

The man scratched his head in puzzlement, it was obvious that he didn't know what to do with me.

"I'm stronger than I look."

"Come on, Al, let her help you. You only have to look at the girl to know that, as my grandmother used to say, she is small but mighty."

The speaker was a dark-haired cowboy with a stack of papers in his hand. I recognized the voice immediately; it was the same guy whose conversation with Zoe I had overheard in the office. He was attractive in a vulgar sort of way, and he knew it; it was obvious that he thought highly of himself.

"I'm Colin." He held out his hand with a charming smile. I shook his hand without returning it and turned back to Al.

The older cowboy finally made up his mind and let me help him push the round bale of hay to the back of the stables. There he explained to me how to unroll it and spread it out properly. I lost track of how many times we repeated the same process, but it was enough to make my leg and lower back ache.

"That's it for today!"

Vance's deep voice startled me. I had been so focused on the exhilarating task of spreading the hay with an iron fork that I hadn't heard him coming.

I straightened my back, which protested with a crack, leaned on the fork handle with both hands, and glared at him. His face was flushed from the cold, and his Stetson and jacket were covered with frost. For the first time that afternoon, I was glad I had to work in the stables; at least it was warm in here.

"Al, Colin, go help Josh finish separating the pregnant heifers from the rest of the herd."

The two men immediately complied, and after wrapping up warm and adjusting their hats so that the strong gusts of wind wouldn't blow them off their heads, they headed out.

"I've been watching you for a while," Vance said once we were alone.

I just lifted my chin defiantly and waited.

"I've noticed that you always avoid going near the animals."

"So what? I did my job, didn't I?"

"You're afraid of them."

I shrugged. "Let's just say that like most *city princesses*," I emphasized the nickname he had given me with sarcasm, "beasts are not my thing. In fact, I had never seen cows or horses up close before."

Vance lifted his hat slightly with one finger in a characteristic gesture and smiled. His eyes were greener than ever. "Didn't they even send you to a farm school when you were little?"

"I remember once, when I was in third grade, they took us to the zoo. But I preferred to stay in the shade of a tree, playing with a little gadget a classmate had lent me. You see," I shook my head in mock regret, "animals and I don't make a good combo."

"Leave that and come with me."

I gripped the fork tighter and frowned. "Where to?"

"Raff always says you are one of the bravest women he knows. I want you to show me he's right."

"Do you really think I'm going to fall for that crude ruse?" I raised a scornful eyebrow.

"Of course." He held out his hand to me with a smile.

This man was really too much, I said to myself exasperated. But I took his hand and let him lead me to one of the stalls.

"Aisha, this is Ranger. Ranger, this is Aisha, I hope you'll be good friends from now on."

The horse moved up and down the black head, which had a white blaze that went from the nostrils to the eyes, as if it understood everything.

"See, he agreed."

Vance pushed me forward slightly, but I dug the heels of my boots into the cement floor and resisted moving any further. Just then, the horse snorted and shook its black mane. Startled, I took a step back and collided with Vance's broad chest pressed against my back.

"He's very... big."

"Are you scared?"

"Of course I'm scared, can't you tell?" I was so focused on the horse, fearing an imminent attack, even though the stall door was locked with a strong bolt, that I didn't notice him grabbing me around the waist.

"The brave are not those who have no fear, but those who have fear but know how to conquer it."

"What's that, a wise proverb from the great Sham Poo?" Despite my wry tone, I swallowed when I realized that Vance had pushed me with his body and that I was now less than fifteen inches from the wooden door. "Let me go! I don't want to...!"

I struggled to get free, but Vance had a firm hold on me.

"Easy, give me your hand."

I hurried to hide it behind my back, but it was no use, for he grabbed my wrist and, without force but firmly, made me place my palm on the animal's muzzle, then covered my hand with his to prevent me from withdrawing it.

Afraid the horse would bite me, I remained completely still, feeling the softness of the animal's skin under my palm and the surprising warmth of Vance's hand.

"See, it's okay," he whispered huskily next to my ear.

Then the strangest thing happened. The horse's big brown eyes fell on mine, and instantly I was the victim of a mysterious spell. Vance released my hand, and I watched nonplussed as it began to caress the silky fur of the animal's forehead of its own accord.

"It's so soft," I said in wonder.

"What did you expect? Spines?"

His teasing remark jolted me out of my rapture and for the first time I was aware that not only was I leaning against this insufferable cowboy's chest, but that strong male hands were resting on my hips as if that was their natural place. Without hesitation, I turned around and pushed him hard, but I failed to move him even half an inch.

I already knew that Vance Bennet was well above average height, but to realize at such close range that I couldn't even brush the top of his shoulder with my head was overwhelming. In recent years – if I didn't count my brother Raff, who was also very tall – the only man with whom I had shared such closeness had been Eric, who, though strong and well-muscled like a good dancer, was slender and barely a couple of inches taller than me. I had felt very comfortable next to him, but the closeness of a guy as big as Vance was crushing. No, I didn't like this feeling of helplessness at all.

I raised my face to him and demanded, "Let go of me right now!"

Obediently, he released me and stepped back.

"Did you like Ranger?"

When I realized that my host, far from harboring malicious intentions about my virtue, was merely trying to make me feel more at ease around the animal, my sudden discomfort vanished and, much more relaxed, I answered with a smile.

"Very much so. It's..." At that moment, Ranger, who apparently didn't like being ignored, brushed his muzzle against my ear, and a nervous laugh escaped me. "It tickles."

Vance stared at me. He had a funny look in his eyes and I suddenly imagined him releasing the thumbs he had hooked into the belt loops of his jeans to put his warm hands on my hips again and pull me tightly against him. I frowned and shook my head, trying to banish such shocking images.

"Good. So, first hurdle over, in the next days I'll teach you how to ride."

It was my turn to stare at him for a long time. As soon as I regained the use of my voice, I shook my head emphatically. "No way. One thing is one thing, but riding this huge beast is quite another."

Vance gave me a lazy smile. "Let me remind you that you work for me now. I need my employees to know how to ride."

"But... I can't, my leg..."

"Nonsense. If you follow my advice, it'll get stronger in no time."

When I heard that, I got really angry. "Yeah, right, after I bust my butt in the kitchen in the morning and work my tail off in these stinking stables in the afternoon, do you think I have time and energy left for dancing? You're not a boss, you're a slave driver of the worst kind!

Ignoring my angry tone, he pondered the question for a few seconds, pressing two fingers to the bridge of his nose. "Hum. You may be right."

"Of course I'm right! I'm always right!"

Once again he ignored my impertinent assertion. "Then choose: kitchen or stables."

"I'd take the stables any day. But what about Fernanda? It's true she needs a helper."

"I like to know that you care about Fernanda."

The attractive wrinkles that reappeared at the corners of his eyes – which were a shade closer to hazel in the electric light – made me realize that that mushy remark had been a mistake. If I wanted Vance to continue to think of me as a nasty bitch that he couldn't wait to kick off his precious ranch, I had to fix this stupid *faux pas* ASAP.

"Actually, what I'm worried about is that dinner won't be ready in time."

He shook his head and laughed and got all cute, which made me even madder. "Aisha Brooks, you're quite a character."

There was no way to make this man angry, I told myself irritably. Again, I couldn't help but compare him to my brother Raff, but this cowboy's cheerfulness was beyond belief.

"Don't worry, though." With a gentleness that was surprising for such a masculine man, Vance brushed aside a strand of hair that had stuck to my lips and tucked it behind my ear. I tensed on the spot and turned my head away to avoid the slight contact, but he remained as calm as if he hadn't noticed my reaction.

"Carol would much rather help Fernanda in the kitchen than work with the animals. She'll be happy to go back to her old job when she gets home from school."

"So working in the kitchen was nothing more than a punishment." I narrowed my eyes accusingly.

"I'm not as bad as you think, princess. I just wanted you and Fernanda to get to know each other a little better." Without further ado, he pulled down his hat and left the stables.

6

That night I slept like a log, and the shrill alarm that woke me rang for more than three minutes before I managed, still half groggy, to reach out and turn it off.

Without showering, I went downstairs for breakfast and, as usual, the three brothers were already there. Vance was finishing his coffee when the kitchen door opened and Miguel, Fernanda's husband, walked in, accompanied by a nasty draft of cold air.

"Al heard wolves at Russ Creek. I've got Ranger saddled up outside the bunkhouse."

Vance put down the cup and stood up at once. Josh had gotten up as well, ready to follow them, but his older brother motioned for him to stay. He put on his jacket, grabbed one of the rifles stored in a wooden gun rack that took up most of the wall by the door and, after checking the ammunition, hurried out with Miguel at his heels.

Intrigued, I walked over to the window, coffee cup in hand, and watched them gallop away. The dark silhouettes of the two riders soon disappeared behind a thick curtain of snowflakes.

I returned to the table and asked with some trepidation, "Are there really wolves?"

"They actually live in Grand Teton National Park, but when the winters are too harsh, it's not uncommon to see them prowling around livestock."

"Vance took a rifle, aren't they protected?"

Josh shrugged. "Yes, they are, although I don't know of any rancher who would stand by and let these beasts attack his cattle."

We finished breakfast quickly. I helped Carol and Fernanda clean up, and was annoyed when Fernanda reacted with unexpected composure when I announced that I would no longer be working in the kitchen. It was clear that 'my boss' had ruined my surprise.

I slowly made my way back up the stairs. In fact, I would almost rather have been busy in the kitchen than face what lay ahead. Back in my room, I pulled up a chair and took out the suitcase I had stored at the top of the closet. I put it on the bed, sat down next to it, and unzipped it. At the bottom were the black leotard and tights I wore for practice, as well as a pair of worn-out ballet shoes. I didn't know why I had put these clothes in the suitcase. I hadn't worn them since the accident and now, as I touched them, the memories of that other life overwhelmed me once again.

I put everything back where it was and slammed the lid shut. I got up and hurried out of the bedroom and into the unoccupied room. I closed the door, leaned against the wood panel with my arms crossed over my chest, and stared at the barre.

"This is ridiculous," I said to myself angrily. "This man has no idea."

I hadn't done any exercise since finishing rehab with the physical therapist, and my leg bothered me whenever I made the slightest effort.

I would forget about it. I would tell this wannabe psychologist cowboy that I wanted to go back to my job in the kitchen. Cutting meat, carrying heavy trays, and scrubbing dozens of pots and pans didn't require me to be in shape.

But he seemed determined that I should try, and though Vance Bennet was no despot or the kind of man to assert himself through fear – in all that time, I had never once seen him angry, and he seemed to be the nicest, easiest guy in the world to get along with – something in those piercing green eyes told me he was used to getting his own way. You only had to see the way Josh, Carol, and the rest of the ranch hands instantly obeyed the slightest of his orders, even though I'd never heard him raise his voice.

"The brave are not those who have no fear, but those who have fear but know how to conquer it."

His words echoed clearly in my head and I closed my eyes. I had been like that until the accident. Ever since I was six years old, when my father left me at Raff's mother's house like a forgotten umbrella, I had fought to get ahead, no matter what it took. I had never given up on anything and had pursued my dreams relentlessly. But the driver who was high on pills when he slammed into my car one rainy November afternoon had changed that, too. Not only had the accident limited my mobility, but it had forced me to give up a glittering dance career, the love of my life... and even my self-respect.

I bit my lip. I could go on like this for the rest of my life, or I could face my fears for once. I would never get back what I had lost, but maybe I could put aside the bitterness that seemed to wrap around me like a second skin and get on with my existence, even if it wasn't the one I had dreamed of.

I went back to my bedroom, stripped completely and stood in front of the mirror. It had been a long time since I had faced my reflection, and although I tried not to look at the horrible scar on my leg, I did not like what I saw. I was extremely thin; the bones of my hips and knees protruded in an unpleasant way, and you could count my ribs. I had lost a lot of muscle mass, and the skin on my arms, thighs, and stomach looked flabby and dull. There was no trace of the well defined muscles that came from endless hours of training. I flexed one arm and tried to show off the muscle, but it was a pathetic attempt.

"This is not going to work," I said aloud, shaking my head without taking my eyes off the skeletal body that seemed to belong to a stranger.

There it was again, the defeatism that had made me crawl like a wandering soul these past few years. I had even given up on attending my brother Raff's unexpected wedding to a Spanish woman he had met during his stay in Madrid, on the pretext that I had not yet recovered, although no one knew better than I that what had really prevented me from taking a flight to accompany him at the most important moment of his life was a mixture of jealousy – I hated to think that Raff would love another woman more than me – and self-pity. This time, however, I was unwilling to succumb to the siren song of self-pity, so I lifted my chin and looked defiantly at my reflection.

"As Calvin Coolidge said, and the ballet teacher repeated *ad nauseam*: 'Nothing in this world can take the place of persistence. Not talent, not genius, not education. Persistence and determination alone are omnipotent.' You," I pointed a menacing finger at my reflection, "will return to the way you were, or at least to a similar version. I swear you will, even if you have to cry tears of blood."

Determined, I walked to the bed, took my leotard, tights and ballet shoes out of the suitcase and put them on. Then I wrapped up warm in the faded sweatshirt that had been with me since high school and left the room.

"Aren't you helping Fernanda today?"

Tessa, standing by the stairs, looked me up and down with her usual disdain. She, on the other hand, was impeccably dressed in smart beige wool slacks and a cashmere turtleneck a few shades lighter. Vance's stepmother was the only person on the ranch who didn't get up at the crack of dawn. I usually only saw her at dinnertime and often wondered what she did the rest of the time.

"No, today your dear stepson gave me the morning off."

She subtly raised her delicate eyebrows in disapproval, and I was not sure if it was because I had used the word 'stepson' or because I had been given the morning off.

"I'm going shopping in Jackson, do you need anything?"

"Aside from a theater, movie theater, museum, or park to stroll through that isn't petrified with ice and a more interesting social life?" I shook my head, "I can't think of anything."

"There's a dive bar in Wilson. I think it's the kind of place where you'd feel right at home."

"Really? I can't wait to go!" I clapped my hands in mock delight..

With a hint of a scornful smile on her painted lips, she started down the stairs and I stepped into the empty room and slammed the door shut.

"Arrogant bitch," I muttered.

I was so angry that I didn't even realize I was starting to warm up until I noticed my forehead was soaked with sweat. I took off the sweatshirt, caressingly tossed it to the floor, and continued with the exercises. Stretching muscles that had not been exercised for centuries was as painful as the most merciless torture. I came close to giving up at least a dozen times, but every time I considered quitting, I heard Vance's voice in my head again, and those words were the best spur.

"On top of everything else, I'm starting to hear voices," I grumbled, panting as I bent my body over my right leg and tried to touch my thigh to my chest. "That's all I needed."

Half an hour later, a trail of painful twinges from the sole of my foot to the groin of my bad leg alerted me that it was time to stop. My leg wasn't the only part of my body that was hurting like hell, even though the muscle soreness hadn't shown up yet. With a groan, I bent down, grabbed the sweatshirt, and pulled it on. I wiped my sweaty face with the sleeve and hobbled to the shower. Every step was an ordeal and I wondered, with increasing concern, if all this exercise hadn't been the final straw for my leg.

After more than twenty minutes under the hot water, I felt a little better. As soon as I got out of the bathroom, the bed started calling me, but I gritted my teeth and resisted the temptation to crawl under the covers. Instead, I decided to go down to the office and see if I could find a book that wasn't about raising cattle.

The door was ajar, so I quietly peeked in and found Zoe sitting at the computer, staring blankly out the window at the small patch of snowy landscape.

"Hi, do you mind if I grab a book?"

Zoe jumped, sending the pile of sheets on her lap flying in all directions and I was forced to suppress an evil grin. "Sorry, did I startle you?"

"Yes, you did, and now I'll have to sort through all these papers again." She kneeled down on the floor and began furiously picking up the sheets.

I responded to her obvious hostility with my most innocent look. "I'm really sorry. Do you want me to help you?"

Suddenly, I had an overwhelming urge to look at all those papers. I could tell I'd spent too much time digging through the dirty laundry of Chuck's clients, I said to myself with a grimace. So I knelt down and began to help her.

"What's all this?"

Zoe didn't seem to find my sudden curiosity suspicious. "These are the accounting spreadsheets. I've to do the accounting with the information I get from the ranch."

"Ugh, looks boring."

I caught a glimmer of suspicion in her honey-colored eyes at my sudden kindness, but she shrugged. "You can't imagine. I'd rather be out there feeding the cattle a thousand times over."

I looked out the window and shuddered at the idea. Even though spring was just around the corner, it was freezing. Zoe continued with her complaints, glad to have a new set of ears to dump them into.

"But Josh, who's supposed to be here, is too busy working side by side with Vance to finish the business administration course he started I don't know how many years ago."

I didn't miss the wistful look on her face as she said, 'Side by side with Vance.' I was sure I had just discovered the crux of the matter.

"I have a degree in business and accounting. If you want, I could help."

Raff had insisted that I combine night classes with ballet, and though it hadn't been easy, I had finally graduated with flying colors from one of those accelerated programs. After the accident, I had dusted off that same degree, and during the months I had spent working at Chuck's agency, I had discovered that I had a special ability to spot at a glance the imaginative financial manipulations that certain businessmen were so fond of making in their accounting books.

"Would you really?" Zoe must have forgotten how jealous she was the first day she saw me chatting with Vance, because she was staring at me like I was an early Christmas present. "I can walk you through the ropes if you…"

"It's not necessary. I'm used to this kind of work."

Just then, the door opened and Brad, another of the cowboys Al had introduced me to at the stables the day before, appeared almost completely covered in frost. Even his long blond hair, tied back in a ponytail, looked like a frozen stick.

"They've caught one of the wolves, Zoe! I rushed over to tell you, I thought you might like to come and see."

"Oh, Brad, I'd love to!" Her eyes sparkled with excitement as she turned to me. I was a little disappointed that she was so trusting; I had long since lost faith in human kindness. "Are you sure you don't mind?"

"Wolves and freezing temperatures." I pretended to shiver. "Positive."

"Thank you, you're a dear." Full of enthusiasm, Zoe grabbed her jacket and hat from the coat rack near the door, and soon the sound of their boots sprinting down the hallway faded.

I picked up the stack of sheets Zoe had left on the floor and sat down in the swivel chair in front of the computer with them in my hand. After making the accounting entries from the information contained in the spreadsheets, I began fiddling with the latest balance sheet, comparing it to previous years. After a few hours, I had discovered some rather curious details.

I turned off the computer, leaned back against the back of the chair, crossed my fingers in my lap, and twiddled my thumbs with a satisfied smile.

"Well, well, well."

The commotion over the capture of the wolf reached the office. I heard shouting, horses neighing, and the engine of one of the ranch trucks. Curious, I bundled up and went outside to see what was going on. At least the snow had stopped falling, but the cold was biting. Happy with my new sheepskin-lined boots, which kept my feet nice and warm,

I walked over to the pickup truck where a crowd of curious onlookers had gathered.

Just then, Vance galloped up and without waiting for the animal to come to a complete stop, he jumped off the horse. "How is he, Miguel?"

"He hasn't woken up yet. Brad is coming with the trailer and I sent Zoe to get the first aid kit."

The latter arrived panting and handed Vance a white briefcase with a red cross in the middle.

"I'll get some soap and water." Again, she hurried off in the direction of the kitchen.

Vance approached the bed of the pickup where the wolf lay motionless and leaned over him, uttering a brutal curse that made my eyes widen.

"It doesn't look like the leg is broken," said Miguel, who had also come closer to get a better look at what his boss was doing.

"No, luckily it's not broken." Vance squeezed the animal's limb hard, trying to stop the blood from gushing out. Once he managed to stop the bleeding, he grabbed a pair of scissors and began cutting the hair around the wound. "At least we got there in time, it wouldn't be the first time I've seen an animal pull and pull on the wire until it tore its leg off."

Hearing that, I felt a little dizzy. Fortunately, Zoe's arrival with a basin of soapy water, a rag, and a pitcher of clean water distracted me.

The cowboy cleaned the wound with a meticulousness worthy of a surgeon, before squirting a good dose of iodine antiseptic to disinfect it thoroughly. At that moment, a second pickup pulling a small metal trailer pulled up next to the first with an unpleasant squeal of brakes.

"Come on, let's lock him up while he's still asleep."

Although Vance never raised his voice, I could tell he was very angry. He needed the help of two more men to lift the huge specimen from the bed of the pickup and onto the trailer.

"That's it." After securing the door, he turned to the crowd of onlookers with his hands on his hips. "I want to know what the hell a snare was doing in the Double B."

The men exchanged confused looks, but no one offered an explanation.

"All right." Vance pursed his lips until they turned white. "I'm only going to say this once, and I'd appreciate it if you'd pass it on, word for word, to those who aren't here."

The green eyes sparkled, and they all avoided his gaze with a guilty look. "I will not tolerate the use of such traps on the Double B. Anyone caught setting one or anything remotely resembling one will be thrown off the ranch immediately. Understood?"

"Got it, boss." The men nodded their heads like obedient children.

"Now get on with whatever it is you were doing." He dismissed them with a wave of his hand, and the cowboys hurried back to the chores they had abandoned.

"Brad, move the trailer away from the stables and corrals, I don't want the pregnant cows getting restless when this beast wakes up," Vance said as he pulled his cell phone from his pocket and began to make a call.

I turned to Josh who was standing next to me and whispered, "I don't get it, why is he so angry? You said yourself that no rancher would stand by and watch his cattle get attacked by wolves. I saw him pick up a rifle before he went out to get it."

Josh smiled, obviously pleased with my interest. "Vance can't stand brutality. Especially when it's directed at the weakest, human or animal. If he had felt the need to shoot, he would have done so without a second thought, even if the rifle had been loaded with a bullet instead of a tranquilizer dart, but he finds this kind of trickery cruel and cowardly."

I looked at my new boss, who was still on the phone. "And what is he going to do with the wolf now?"

Much to my regret, I was fascinated by Josh's brother's amazing self-control. It was obvious that he was terribly angry, yet he retained a tight grip on his emotions. Suddenly, I wondered what would happen the day he lost some of that control, and I shuddered. I just hoped I wasn't around to see it.

"He's calling the Rangers to come get him."

"Ah." My hands were starting to feel numb from the cold, so I said goodbye to Josh and walked back to the house. I didn't see either of them again until much later.

My shift at the stables was finally over. With a sigh of relief, I leaned the shovel I had been using to clean the horses' stalls against one of the walls and felt an ominous creak as I tried to straighten my stiff spine. I held my neck with one hand and tilted my head to one side. God, my whole body ached.

"Tired? I saw that you were limping."

I turned to see Vance looking at me with a lazy smile. He was leaning against the door of the stall directly opposite, the sole of one of his boots against the wood and his thumbs hooked into the belt loops of his pants. As usual, his hat was tilted back slightly, giving him the air of a libertine bandit. I wondered how long he had been standing there.

"I don't like being spied on."

He slapped his forehead, feigning melancholy. "I wonder if I'll ever be able to remember all the things you don't like."

"I'm afraid I don't have time for this kind of nonsense." I grabbed the coat from one of the harness hooks and began to put it on.

"Not so fast."

"I'm done with my shift. You can check the stalls if you want, I don't think they've ever been half as shiny." I raised my nose in clear defiance.

"Your nose is too small and upturned for that gesture to be effective."

"It's not upturned!" Offended, I brought my hand to the aforementioned appendage. Actually, I had always wished for a bigger nose; mine had a childlike quality that detracted from my dignity.

He must have realized that he had touched on a sensitive spot, because he immediately changed the subject. "I told you I'd teach you to ride, remember?"

"Let's leave that for another day. I'm exhausted."

"Don't worry, we won't be long today, and I promise I'll try to get here sooner tomorrow. This wolf business has kept me very busy."

Annoyed, I hit the cement floor with my boot and had to bite my lip to keep from moaning in pain. "I don't care what you say. I don't want to ride. You can't make me!"

"No?" He arched an eyebrow lazily.

"No!"

Vance loosened his fingers from the belt loops and pulled his hat down to his eyebrows. He slowly straightened up, never taking his eyes off me, and with a movement so quick I didn't even have time to guess his intentions, he grabbed me by the waist and placed me on top of Ranger's saddle, who was waiting a few feet away, nibbling on some straw.

Immediately, I clung to the horn of the chair with all my might. "Put me down! Put me down now!" Although I was terrified, I didn't dare to scream for fear that the creature would go berserk and run away with me on top.

"Calm down, princess." He grabbed the horse's mane, put his left foot in the stirrup, and jumped up behind me with an agility that was amazing for a man his size. "Come on, relax."

"How can I relax? I'm more than six feet away from a concrete floor that looks like it's going to hurt when this beast rears up and I land headfirst on it, or imagine if it starts kicking and…"

I didn't even finish verbalizing my long list of fears before I clung even tighter to the horn, and only when I realized that the movement I felt behind me was the soft laughter of my torturer did I dare open my eyes and give him a murderous look over my shoulder.

"Don't laugh at me!"

"I know, I know, you don't like it."

Vance leaned over me a little more, grabbed the reins hanging loosely around the horse's neck and held them in his left hand. Gently, he kicked Ranger's sides with his heels, forcing him forward down the corridor that separated the rows of stalls.

"Get used to the rub of the saddle against your thighs, to Ranger's movement. Don't fight it. Let yourself go, like in a dance." The deep voice so close to my ear, accompanied by the warmth of his chest against my back and the pressure of compact thighs against my own, was soothing and I began to relax. I tried to do as he said and let the rhythmic swaying of the animal carry me along.

When we reached the end of the stables, Vance gave the reins a slight tug to turn the horse. "Now you take the reins."

I struggled to open my stiff fingers to let go of the horn and took the reins as he instructed. Holding on to two thin strips of leather with one hand was much more frightening than clinging to the horn saddle. I felt completely unsteady and had to make a superhuman effort to resist the urge to pull back hard.

"Don't pull, Ranger's got a tender mouth," the cowboy warned me, as if he had read my mind. "Just nudge him lightly with your heel, like this, see, and he'll know what to do."

I don't know how long we walked up and down the corridor, but by the time Vance stopped the horse, I had lost the fear I had felt at first.

"Not bad for a city princess."

He jumped down and, without asking my permission, grabbed me around the waist again, lifted me out of the saddle, and set me down on the ground. I was used to Eric lifting me into the air as if I weighed no more than a feather, even though I could feel the tension in his muscles. I had the feeling, however, that Vance didn't require any effort.

As soon as I put my foot on the ground, I couldn't help but wince.

"Do you want me to carry you?" He asked concernedly.

"No way, cowboy. I don't like being carried around like a sack of potatoes," I emphasized the 'don't' part.

He gave me one of those slow smiles that revealed his very white teeth. "I promise you, I'd be much more gentle."

"Don't insist." I buttoned my coat all the way up.

"So how did you like riding Ranger?"

"Let's just say it wasn't too bad. I'm willing to let you teach me to ride, but I want the horse all to myself. I don't like to share." I said with the tone of a true princess.

I pulled my hat on tightly and limped away with my head held high.

"All right, old man," I heard him say. Curious, I turned to see him patting Ranger's neck affectionately before bending down to loosen the saddle girth. "It's clear this tiny princess is going to give us a lot of trouble."

7

From then on, the weeks followed a very similar pattern. In the mornings, I went through the exercise routines that had been part of my life for so many years, and although the pain was almost unbearable at first, I began to notice some improvement. I was more agile, my stride was more confident, and I had even dared to do some simple pirouettes. The daily work in the stables and the riding lessons also contributed to the strengthening of my leg.

In addition, so much physical activity had given me an appetite. I was hungry all the time and had gained back some of the pounds I had lost over the past few years. The new jeans fit seductively on my hips, which had lost their straight angles to the point that I had caught several glances of male admiration directed at my butt while doing my chores. Of course, at the end of the day, I would fall into bed like a sack of lead and not move until my cell phone alarm went off the next morning.

The time between the end of practice and lunch was usually spent helping Zoe in the office. At least that was what she thought when she said goodbye to me with a grateful smile to go do the kind of things she thought were a thousand times more interesting and appropriate on a cattle ranch.

Once I was alone, I wasted no time. As soon as I was done with the routine paperwork, I began to sift through the accounting data from the last few years. After several attempts, I had managed to get Zoe's password – she wasn't very careful with computer security either – and I had been poring over the ranch's ledger for several days.

Colin, the cowboy in charge of filling out the auxiliary accounting spreadsheets that Zoe then had to feed into the computer, had shown up at the office a couple of times. The first time, he was very surprised to see me there instead of Zoe, but as soon as I mentioned that I was helping her with some of the bookkeeping, he put on his most seductive smile and started flirting with me.

At first I tried to brush him off with some rudeness, but the guy was very persistent. So I decided it would be more productive to change tactics and play along. Whenever Colin showed up at the office or we ran into each other in the stables, I made it a point to return his smile, chat with him, and ask him a few questions along the way, trying not to seem too inquisitive. Cleverly – Chuck always sent me ahead to talk to the shady characters we were investigating –

I managed to elicit some information from him, but as soon as I noticed that he began to get defensive, I had no choice but to abandon my inquiries and return to the meaningless chatter full of more or less veiled sexual innuendo that the man found irresistible.

The bad news was that the Double B Ranch was a miniature universe populated by a collection of beings who, in my opinion, were nothing more than a bunch of bored busybodies, and our sudden 'friendship' did not go unnoticed by anyone.

I had to endure, trying not to grit my teeth, the well-meaning advice of Zoe, several years my junior, who warned me of the dangers of associating with philandering cowboys; the snide remarks of Fernanda, who said much the same thing and the scornful smiles of Tessa, who, despite spending more time in Jackson than at the ranch, was always up on the latest gossip. Even Carol worried about my possible heartbreak. But the last straw came when 'my boss' dared to call me to order during one of our daily riding lessons.

We were in the small arena next to the stables. Vance had found me a beautiful, noble chestnut mare that I fell in love with at first sight, and surprisingly, I immediately began to make progress, to the point that my instructor often had to restrain my reckless excesses.

"Can I gallop now?" I was bored with going round and round at a trot.

"No, not yet."

Vance stood in the center of the arena, watching my progress with a long dressage whip in his hand.

"We've done this a thousand times."

"Stand straighter, reins longer."

I straightened my back even more and adjusted the reins in my hand, resisting the urge to stick my tongue out at him. This man had a gift for making me react in ways I hadn't since my days as a rebellious teenager.

"At this rate, I'll never get out of this boring riding arena."

"Stop complaining and don't bow your head."

I obeyed, gritting my teeth. If it weren't for the fact that he was one of the best teachers I'd ever had, I'd have told him to go to hell a few times by now.

"What is it with you and Colin?"

The question surprised me so much that I unintentionally tugged on the reins, causing the mare to change her trot into a long stride.

"None of your business," I replied angrily as I recovered from the shock, unconsciously digging my heels into Maya's flanks as she returned to her light trot. "I don't like being questioned about my private life."

"Stop giving contradictory orders! Poor Maya doesn't know whether to trot, walk or do a few cartwheels."

I leaned over and stroked the light brown mane, feeling a little guilty, but immediately raised my head defiantly. "You have no right to ask me personal questions."

"You're my employee, I don't want you going into a decline because you're in a dead-end relationship with a cowboy who has no intention of settling down. Your performance would suffer."

"You are not my father and you have no authority over me." I was angry, but I controlled the volume of my voice so as not to frighten the mare. "For your information, I'll have whatever relationship I want, future or no future, without asking your permission."

"Have you let go of Eric yet?"

This time the jerk was so sharp that the mare stopped dead in her tracks and I was almost thrown over her head. Instantly, Vance was at my side, and with a certain roughness, he slipped my foot back into the stirrup.

"I've told you a thousand times, Aisha Brooks, when you ride a horse, you cannot be distracted for a minute. Even the most docile animal can react unexpectedly and take you by surprise."

I shot him an indignant look. "It was you who broke my concentration with your questions. Who spoke to you...?" I noticed that my voice wasn't very steady and cleared my throat before continuing, "Who told you about Eric?"

"I saw you with him that night, remember? Raff told me that you two had ended badly, although I didn't know the details. He told me that it was the breakup of your relationship that finally brought you down."

I bit my lip hard; I had suddenly lost the ability to retort with my usual cockiness.

"I'm tired," I said quietly, and without waiting for him to help me as he always did, I got off the horse by myself, taking care not to land on my bad leg. "I'll take Maya to her stall."

I reached for the horse's reins, but he didn't pull away.

"Aisha…"

His voice was filled with compassion, so I kept my head down. I couldn't stand people looking at me with pity. But Vance put a finger under my chin and gently forced me to look into his eyes.

"I can see that neither Colin nor... No one," I didn't miss the slight hesitation, but immediately forgot it, "has anything to do with you."

"None of your business," I repeated, though this time the words were free of the fire with which I had spoken them earlier.

After staring at me for a few seconds, Vance released me and stepped aside. "Don't worry about Maya, I'll take care of her."

I nodded and walked away with my head down. When I got to the house, I stopped by the kitchen where Fernanda was humming and stirring the contents of the pot on the stove. I told her that I was going to make myself a sandwich. I was too tired to wait for dinner, I explained, and I wanted to go to sleep as soon as possible.

The cook frowned at my dull look and, for once, said nothing. She made me a huge triple-decker sandwich herself, which she left on the table, then took a glass from the cupboard and filled it to the brim with cold water. I thanked her and began to eat in silence, oblivious to the worried looks the woman kept giving me. When I finished, I washed up what I had used, thanked her again and said goodbye.

"Hum," I heard her say to herself, "I don't like to see the *señoritinga* so meek. She's not going to get sick, is she? We'll have to keep an eye on her."

Back in my room, I put on my pajamas, brushed my teeth, lay on my back on the mattress, and whispered the same words that Vance had said, "Have you forgotten Eric yet?"

Forget Eric. Forget the only man I ever made love to. Forget the strong, wiry body I had run my fingertips over from every angle. Forget the feel of the blond hair – even softer than mine – that he wore in a bun. Forget the passion we had shared for each other and especially for dancing.

I burst into a laugh that had nothing joyful about it.

Forget... I could never forget.

The next day I did my practice as usual, but when I was done, instead of picking up my clothes and showering as usual, I changed the playlist on my phone and instead of the banging music I had been listening to, the first chords of *Don Quixote* began to play.

I stood still, holding on to the barre, letting the music I loved so much flow through me from head to toe, filling me with energy until I suddenly let go and started dancing. I didn't even have to think about the steps; after years and years and thousands of days and millions of hours of practice, they were branded with fire in my body.

The music transported me back to the ballet hall in Los Angeles and I forgot everything else. Completely lost in the dance, I launched into a *grand jeté* as I had done countless times before. More than five feet off the ground, with one leg fully extended forward and the other behind me, I felt myself flying, but just then, unwanted reality kicked in with its usual rudeness, and as I landed my bad leg on the floor, it gave way and I fell face first to the floor.

But it wasn't the blinding pain that shot from my instep to my groin that made me burst into heartbreaking sobs. What tore me apart was the realization that I would never get back what I had lost: not the ballet, not the applause, and certainly not Eric.

I barely noticed as strong arms lifted me from the floor and forced me to lie against a massive chest covered in a soft flannel shirt. With my fists clenched against that same chest, I continued to cry with an intensity I had never experienced before. The person holding me said not a word, just held me tightly as my body shook with sobs so violent I thought they would break me in half.

It wasn't until much later that my crying began to subside. I was still lying against that welcoming chest, eyes closed, fists clenched. Every now and then an uncontrolled hiccup would escape me, making me wince, but despite the dulling of my brain, I began to take in more details of what was going on around me.

The first thing I noticed was that I was sitting on someone's lap, and the dampness of the fabric on which my cheek rested contrasted with the warmth radiating from the skin it covered. Then I caught the scent of the person holding me; a mixture of soap, shaving cream, leather and horse that was all too familiar.

"Vance?" I whispered, too exhausted to open my eyelids.

I had no idea what the owner of the Double B was doing here at this hour, but I didn't feel like asking.

"Who did you think I was?"

"Nobody."

"You seem disappointed."

I shrugged, but continued to lean against him.

"How's your leg?"

"Fine."

"Don't lie to me, Aisha, I saw the whole thing and it wasn't a good fall. I know you must be in a lot of pain."

I didn't deny it. I didn't lift my head either. It felt good just lying against him. The warmth of his body was comforting and I didn't feel like talking.

"Aisha..." But I knew that he would insist until he got satisfactory answers.

"I've been hurt enough to know when it's serious. This is nothing."

"Then tell me why you were crying like something was broken inside you."

And suddenly I found myself telling him what I had never told anyone, not even my brother Raff. I told him about the moment when I woke up disoriented in the hospital room; about the insane pain that even the strongest painkillers could not alleviate; about the diplomatic speech with which the surgeon who had operated on me and saved my leg told me that my career as a dancer was over; about the pity I saw in the eyes of my colleagues who came to visit me; about the way Eric, with whom I had lived for several years, immediately averted his gaze when his eyes happened to fall on my injured leg; about the endless months I spent confined to the hospital.

About the endless hours I spent locked in the small apartment we shared, staring at the wall, trying not to think; about the first steps on crutches; about the pain, the terrible pain that never stopped; about my despair; about the pathetic way I dragged myself through the following months, hooked on painkillers, with a dull head; about the torturous treatment my brother Raff paid for me in an expensive detoxification clinic frequented by many celebrities; about my relapse; about my new hospitalization.

About the oath I had sworn and signed in blood – literally, because I had stuck a needle in my thumb, just like when I was a kid – that I would make it through this and pay Raff back every cent; about my work at that sleazy detective agency, which nonetheless brought me out of my lethargy; about the day I came home and found Eric in my bed with Antea, one of the company dancers and my most direct rival, and understood that he had done it on purpose. I told him about the blank look on my boyfriend's face when I accused him of being too cowardly to tell me to my face, and he blurted out, without a trace of emotion, that dance was his life and he couldn't bear to watch my clumsy movements one more day...

When I got to the false suicide attempt and the judge's decision to send me to the ranch, I stopped; he already knew that part of the story, and I had a sore throat from talking so much.

Then there was a deep silence, and I stayed very still, feeling the same relief as if this had been a gigantic pimple that, when it burst, had suddenly expelled all the pus it had accumulated inside.

It was quite a while before Vance, who had not said a word all that time, spoke in a light tone, "I'd like to make you a proposition, but I don't want you to take it the wrong way."

"A proposition?" I opened my eyes; I was suddenly vaguely curious.

"I know you would have preferred Eric to be in my place a thousand times over, and of course I understand that. As much as he is a bastard son of a bitch," I stiffened, but he didn't apologize, "the person you love is not at your side to comfort you."

"Congratulations, you're very smart to have figured that out," I replied with a trace of my former acidity.

"I volunteer."

"Volunteer?" I wrinkled my nose, puzzled. What was the man talking about now?

"To comfort you."

"I'm fine." I shrugged.

"I am very good at comforting."

This absurd conversation after the previous drama made me sit up and look at his face. "What exactly are you offering me?"

Now it was his turn to shrug. "Nothing really. The usual: a hug, a kiss..."

"A kiss." I looked at him confused. "Do you want to kiss me?"

"Just to help you get over your sadness."

Did that cowboy think I was born yesterday? I was about to get up and go to my bedroom to lick my wounds in peace when it occurred to me that Eric was the only man I had ever kissed in my life. It sounded ridiculous at my age, but the dance world was very female. Most of the male dancers were gay, though I could tell by the way the few I knew who weren't looked at me that they found me attractive. Of course, that was a few centuries ago; lately I felt about as attractive as a fleshless zombie.

I looked curiously at Vance's mouth. It was wider than Eric's and had thinner lips, giving an overall impression of firmness, accentuated by the energetic chin with an almost imperceptible dimple in the center. He must not have shaved in the morning, because unlike my ex, who barely had to go through the razor a couple of times a fortnight, there was some dark stubble on his cheeks that was missing the day before. All in all, it was an attractive mouth. You could even say it was a 'kissable' mouth.

"Have you decided or are you just going to watch?"

"All right."

"All right?"

"You can kiss me."

Vance put his big hands on either side of my face and stared at me. "You're pale and your eyes are very red."

"You're supposed to comfort me, not make me feel worse."

"You're right, I'm sorry. You know," he continued, "you're one of the most beautiful women I've ever seen in my life."

"There's no need to exaggerate either. Are you going to kiss me or not? I don't have all day, and I guess you don't either."

"Yeah, sure. I'm definitely going to."

He leaned in but stopped a few inches from my mouth. "You know, Aisha?" his warm breath brushed my lips, "these things work better if you relax a little."

I realized that I had squeezed my eyelids tightly shut and my fists pressed against his chest, so I took his advice and tried to relax. Then his mouth rested on mine with extraordinary delicacy and I noticed he was smiling. I was annoyed that he was laughing at me, but I dismissed the idea of getting angry with him and concentrated on the kiss.

The first thing I noticed was the softness of his lips. Vance was an imposing man, and although I hadn't given the matter much thought, I had expected his kisses to have a hint of roughness to them. Instead, the feeling was quite brotherly; like kissing a good friend or Raff.

Without realizing it, I relaxed a little more and put my hands on his shoulders. They were very broad shoulders and I could feel the hardness of the muscles under the flannel shirt. Vance tangled his fingers in my hair and pulled me closer until our breasts touched. I didn't resist; it was nice to feel the warmth of his virile body against mine. I clasped my hands behind his neck, and the tip of Vance's tongue playfully traced the outline of my mouth, enticing me to part my lips, and then…

Truth is, I never really knew what happened next. Suddenly, the calm, the peace, even the slight drowsiness that I had been experiencing up to that moment was blown away. Now the cowboy's mouth was wrapped around mine as his tongue explored the soft wetness inside with a passion that was as sudden as it was unexpected, instantly overriding any rational thought. All of a sudden, I was no longer a vaguely passive woman analyzing every single sensation. I was so aroused that the sensitivity of my nerve endings had become almost painful. Startled by such a reaction, which I would not have predicted in a thousand years, I pressed my palms against Vance's chest and pushed him away.

Immediately he stopped kissing me, threw his head back and looked into my eyes. His eyes were greener than ever and I had no idea what was going through his mind at that moment.

"Do you feel better now?" he smiled solicitously.

He looked so calm and self-possessed that I wondered if I was the only one who had felt that searing heat. Maybe it was all in my head. The truth was that it had been a long time since I had kissed anyone.

"Yes, much better, thank you," I said as politely as if he had just handed me a plate of strawberries at one of those Jane Austen al fresco parties.

Vance lifted me from his lap and sat me down on the floor before standing up and leaning over to help me. "Can you put your foot down?"

"I told you it's nothing." As soon as I put some weight on my bad leg, I felt a painful cramp that belied my blunt statement.

"I see." He clicked his tongue disapprovingly, bent down and took me in his arms.

"I can walk! I don't like..."

"You don't like being helped." He finished the sentence for me, as annoying as ever.

I bit my lip but wrapped my arms around his neck. "I wasn't going to say that. I was going to say that I don't like being carried".

Vance opened the door to my room without letting go. "Well, it's pretty much the same thing, isn't it?"

He laid me down on the bed with extreme gentleness. "You will not be working in the stables today and riding lessons are canceled until further notice."

"I'm fine, really…" I started to protest again, but he put a finger under my chin and forced me to lift my face.

"Lie down and rest. I'll check on you at noon. If you're not better by then, I'm taking you to Jackson to have your leg looked at, understand?"

It was as clear as day that he wasn't going to budge, so I was forced to nod. Sensing my reluctance, he smiled and headed for the door.

"Vance…"

My voice stopped him in his tracks, and with the doorknob in his hand, he turned to look at me.

"Thank you."

The lines at the corners of his eyes became a little more pronounced, but he didn't say a word. He just opened the door and walked out.

8

I barely saw Vance for the next few days, which made me quite happy. I couldn't help but feel a little uncomfortable in his presence, even though I pretended that what had happened in the fake ballet studio – both my pathetic confession and the surprise kiss – had never happened.

As Al said, spring calving had begun, and everyone on the ranch was busy. Calves were usually born when the herd was resting, so the trick was to feed the pregnant cows well into the night so they would calve first thing in the morning. With this system, the workers could at least get some sleep between rounds and, if complications arose, avoid having to drag the veterinarian out of bed at ungodly hours. Still, Vance had to get up from the table twice in the middle of dinner to help a first-time heifer that was having trouble.

At all hours of the day and night, there were always large quantities of hot coffee and broth in the kitchen. Fernanda and Carol couldn't keep up with making sandwiches and hamburgers either, because with so much overtime, the workers were always hungry. I was glad to be out of the kitchen; cooking had never been my forte.

But I also worked steadily. As I had told Vance the day he caught me crying, it was just the bruise; so after a day's rest I was back to my routine and felt no more discomfort in my leg than usual. One of my duties was to clean the corrals where the heifers were kept. Every two days, with the help of a shovel and a wheelbarrow, I had to pick up the remains of straw and manure and put down a new bed of clean straw.

At first the heifers frightened me and I tried to work as far away from the herd as possible. One of them, more curious and braver than the others, followed me everywhere and the moment I let my guard down, bumped into my rear end and threw me to the ground. The first time, I got up quickly and ran to safety behind the fence. From there I threatened the animal with the shovel while trying to ignore the uncontrollable guffaws of Al and Colin, who had witnessed my humiliation.

But after the third time I ended up on my knees in the mud, I made a deal with her: I would bring her a little salt every day, and in exchange, Maleficent – that was the name I had given her – would stop playing that annoying game. Al, who always tried to be near me when I approached the heifer corral, had laughed heartily at this serious conversation; but to his surprise, little Maleficent understood right away, and from then on she just followed me from one side of the corral to the other, her loving brown eyes fixed on me.

So when she didn't come running to greet me a week later, I was worried. I approached her and held out my hand with a little salt in the palm, but that day she refused. I watched her as I finished spreading a new bed of straw in the corral. She was acting weird. She walked aimlessly from one side of the corral to the other, and I often saw her pawing or digging in the ground. Worried, I told Al and he immediately came over to examine her.

"There is no dilation of the birth canal. I think Maleficent has a few more days to go."

"She's acting very strange."

"That's normal for first-time moms, don't worry." Whistling, Al continued with his chores, but I was still restless.

There was no riding lesson that afternoon either. One of the horses had slipped on a patch of ice and the cowboy riding it had been thrown and broken his leg. Vance had to take him to the hospital in Jackson; from there he called Josh and told him it would be a while and not to wait for him for dinner.

I looked at the clock on my phone; it was one in the morning and I was still tossing and turning in bed. I pulled back the sheets, got up, got dressed, and left the bedroom, trying not to make any noise. I pulled up my collar and walked to the stables, huddling in the cold. The light of the full moon illuminated the path, making the snow-covered ground seem ghostly. As I approached the corral, I heard a distressed mooing and knew something was wrong. Maleficent, standing in a corner, was mooing frantically and snapping her tail. I slowly approached and stroked her neck, trying to calm her down, but it was obvious that something was wrong.

"Stay here," I said stupidly, as if the poor thing was going anywhere. "I'll go get help."

I ran back into the house, climbed the stairs two at a time, and knocked on Vance's bedroom door, but there was no answer. Impatiently, I turned the knob and walked over to the bed with the moonlight coming through the window as my only guide.

"Vance! Vance, wake up!" I whispered, but the cowboy didn't stir.

I came closer and shook his shoulder. "Vance!"

"Aisha?" he asked sleepily.

But before I had time to explain what I was up to, he grabbed me around the waist and flung me onto the bed.

"What a pleasant surprise," he said before getting on top of me and starting to kiss me passionately.

Stunned by his unexpected maneuver, it took me a few minutes to react, although my free-floating mind had enough time to come to the conclusion that Vance Bennet was sleeping naked despite the cold. When I finally got my mind back, I turned my face away and pushed him hard; his bare chest radiated an incredible warmth. By God, this man was a human oven!

"Let go of me, Vance!" I ordered, though I noticed my voice was not as firm as I would have liked. "That's not why I'm here."

Vance propped himself up on his forearms and although he was no longer kissing me, his body still covered mine and his face was too close. "No? My, what a terrible mess. Forgive me, I don't know what to say. I am deeply ashamed." Despite his apologetic tone and the fact that I couldn't make out his expression in the darkness, I knew the idiot was smiling.

"It's Maleficent."

"Your friend the cow?"

Apparently, news was flying around the ranch.

"I think she's in labor and in trouble."

Vance immediately became serious and jumped to his feet. "I made the rounds on my way back from the hospital and it was quiet."

He quickly began to dress, and I thanked the heavens for the dim light that prevented me from seeing his nakedness. It was clear that the concept of modesty was of little importance to this brazen cowboy.

"Come on." He leaned over me, grabbed my hand, and helped me up. We ran back toward the corral, Vance leaping over the fence while I followed more slowly. When we reached the heifer, we saw that the calf's front legs were already sticking out of the birth canal.

"Hum." This simple sound seemed to me to be an ominous omen.

"What's wrong?" I was very worried, I could tell that the animal was suffering, and although I imagined that this was somewhat normal under the circumstances, I was not sure.

"The calf is big and it's Maleficent's first calving."

"Then do something, quickly!"

"For now, we'll just have to wait." Wait? For God's sake, what kind of solution was that? I opened my mouth to protest, but he stopped me with a wave of his hand. "I'll prepare some things while you go to the kitchen and get a thermos of hot coffee. It's going to be a long night."

I nodded, glad to have something to do, and flew to the kitchen. When I returned, I saw that Vance had brought over a basin full of water, some plastic jars and a rather worn leather doctor's bag, and was now sitting on the straw with his back to the fence and his eyes closed. I realized he must be exhausted and felt a little guilty, but when I heard Maleficent's mooing, my guilt vanished instantly.

"Are you just going to stay there?"

The cowboy slowly opened his eyes and gave me an inscrutable look. "Ah, coffee, just what I needed." With a satisfied look, he tipped his hat back as if he hadn't heard my tone.

Pressing my lips together to keep from snapping at him again, I sat down next to him. I unscrewed the cap and poured some coffee into the plastic cup. Take it,' I held it out to him with a not too friendly expression. He took a long sip, eyes closed, and handed it back to me.

"Delicious, drink some." I looked at the glass hesitantly and he added mockingly, "I don't think you'll get poisoned. Remember, we've already exchanged spit a few times."

I noticed that I was blushing, but I preferred not to answer. I took the cup and drank. Vance was right, it was delicious and the hot coffee comforted me.

We were silent again. I was fidgeting, and he must have noticed, because he put his arm around my shoulders and said with that calmness that got on my nerves, "We have to wait a little longer. If we see that the delivery is not successful, we will have to intervene."

He leaned his head against one of the fence posts, pulled his hat down over his eyes and closed them. I thought it was very unkind of him to doze off as if he didn't care, but for once I didn't say anything, nor did I free myself from his arm. It was cold in the stables and his body gave off more calories than a radiator.

"I'm going to check on things." His deep voice startled me and I realized that I had fallen asleep curled up against him.

Vance got up, walked over to Maleficent, who was lying on the straw, and examined her. I saw him shake his head and my stomach tightened.

"I'm afraid this is as far as this goes." He unbuttoned his jacket, took it off and hung it on one of the poles. Then he opened the doctor's bag and took out a plastic glove, which reached almost to his shoulder, and put it on. With a sponge, he washed the area where the calf was protruding with soap and water, before applying lubricant to the hand and arm covered by the glove.

"You're going to have to help me."

"Me?" I was horrified, but this man without feelings didn't care.

"Put on some gloves."

I realized this was not a good time to argue, so I also unbuttoned my coat and took it off. Then I pulled a pair of regular latex gloves out of the leather bag. My hands were shaking so badly that I almost dropped one of them. When I finally got each finger in place, I turned to Vance, and when I saw that his hand and a good part of his arm were lost in some corner of Maleficent's interior, I couldn't help but shiver.

"We're lucky. The calf is well positioned, but its hips are stuck in the mother's pelvis. Help me turn Maleficent on her side."

Pushing, we managed to roll the cow onto her side and I exhaled in relief. I wasn't cold anymore, on the contrary, I was sweating and had to wipe my forehead with the sleeve of my sweater.

"And now?"

"Now the calf has more room to rotate a little and free its hips." He put his hand back inside the cow, which was mooing desperately, to check the position. "I think that's it. Hand me the obstetric loop."

What was this guy thinking? That I had spent my life delivering cows? Frantically, I rummaged through the doctor's bag and found some kind of metal ties. "These?"

"Yes, of course." He gestured at me impatiently, as if I were the most ignorant person he had ever met. If it hadn't been for the fact that poor Maleficent was having a terrible time, I would have made it very clear to him what I thought of know-it-alls like him.

He tied a loop around each of the calf's legs and held one out to me. "When I tell you, pull."

Despite my nervousness, I followed his instructions to the letter. We took turns pulling, matching the rhythm of the heifer's thrusts, until with one final push the calf shot out, wrapped in the placenta. Vance crouched down beside him, freed him from the sticky bag, and began wiping fluid from his nose.

"Take a handful of straw and rub his chest."

I obeyed at once, and a few seconds later the animal began to breathe. "It's breathing!"

I heard the pitiful mooing of the mother who had risen. Immediately, Vance picked up the calf, placed it beside her, and Maleficent began cleaning the newborn with vigorous licks. A few minutes later, almost dry, it managed to stand up after several attempts and began to suckle eagerly.

I watched the little miracle in amazement, still unable to believe what a starring role Vance and I had played in all of this. At that moment I felt the weight of the cowboy's hands on my shoulders, turned my face to him and gave him a tired but happy smile.

"We made it."

"We made it," he smiled back and turned me around until we were facing each other.

For a few eternal seconds I thought he was going to kiss me and I felt a strange tingling in the pit of my stomach. His green eyes were fixed on my lips, and his head, covered by the ever-present Stetson, began to descend inch by inch toward me. I closed my eyelids, anticipating the touch of his lips, but suddenly he released me and stepped back.

"We'd better try to get a few hours sleep before dawn."

I snapped my eyes open, surprised by the frustration I felt. Vance Bennet didn't interest me in the least, I told myself angrily. He was nothing more to me than the man who had accepted my presence on his ranch for a few months as a favor to an old friend. I should not forget that. I still hadn't recovered from Eric, and I certainly wasn't ready to have an insubstantial affair with a cowboy with whom I had nothing in common, no matter how attractive he was, despite his overgrown beard and tired appearance after spending most of the night delivering a calf.

"You're right, I'm exhausted."

I helped him pick everything up and we walked in silence to the house.

"Good night."

"Good night." I went into my bedroom without looking at him and closed the door.

For a few days I avoided Vance as much as possible. I knew I should talk to him as soon as possible about what I had discovered while going through the books, but with all the chaos at the ranch and how little I wanted to make a fuss now that I was starting to feel more comfortable there, I had put it off for days. Besides, like my brother, the cowboy wasn't exactly on my popularity list. However, I couldn't deny that he had been very good to me and that I owed him something.

So I went to his office one night after dinner. I knocked on the door a few times and entered without waiting for an answer. Vance looked up from the paperwork he was reviewing, and I was surprised to see he was wearing black-rimmed glasses.

"Come in, Aisha." He invited me with irony as he watched me pull up a chair and sit down in front of him.

"I need to talk to you." And without missing a beat, I added, dead curious, "Since when do you wear glasses?"

He ran a hand through his disheveled hair and smiled. "I can see very well from a distance, but I've needed glasses to read since I was a teenager."

"They don't suit you at all," I said, shaking my head even though it wasn't true. "They don't match your thirty percent Sioux blood."

"You're right, I'm afraid it's my twenty percent German blood that's to blame. Bunch of studious, boring engineers. What did you want to talk to me about?"

Without answering, I pointed to the pile of papers. "You look very busy. I can come back another time."

He leaned back in his chair and rubbed the bridge of his nose with a weary sigh. "I have such a backlog of paperwork that I don't think a few minutes chatting with you will make any difference. By the way, I wanted to thank you. Zoe told me you're helping her with the accounts."

I shrugged. "Unlike her, I like doing it."

"You're right, she doesn't like it at all, and I barely have time to check her work. I've been trying for months to find someone to do the paperwork while Josh finishes his degree. The bad news is that the Double B is apparently synonymous with the end of the world for young people with aspirations. As anyone can see, my brother is in no hurry to finish his degree, so I convinced Zoe that this would be a temporary thing, but…"

"But she realized that it's going to take quite a while, and she's not happy about it at all." For a change, I was the one who finished the sentence for him.

"Exactly."

"That's why I wanted to talk to you. I've noticed some strange movements in the books."

He looked at me with a frown and I realized that for once I had managed to surprise him. "Strange movements?"

I decided not to beat around the bush. "Since a few years ago, the mortality rate on the ranch has increased by almost five percent for no apparent reason. As far as I could find out, the Double B has not been hit hard by cattle diseases recently. Also, the number of cattle used for domestic consumption has tripled without a corresponding increase in the number of employees."

"Do you have proof?"

I moved around the table to the other side, pushed his swivel chair aside, and began typing rapidly at the computer. Vance looked over my shoulder to see the screen, and the scent of leather, horse, fresh air… in short, his scent, went straight into my head. Annoyed, I told myself to stop fooling around and concentrate on what I was doing.

I showed him the analysis I had done with the data from the last five years. We spent nearly an hour going over the questionable accounting and the ranch's logbook. Vance was very thorough, wanting to make sure that my suspicions were not based on a few minor errors. By the end, he seemed convinced.

"It's not hard to imagine who's behind this." He pursed his lips, you could tell he was very angry, but as usual he hadn't raised his voice.

"Colin?"

"Yes, Colin, with someone's help, of course. I have my suspicions about that too."

"But he's related to you, isn't he?"

"Very distantly, his father was a second cousin of mine. Colin has been moving from ranch to ranch for years, and it was his mother who begged me to give him a permanent job. He's a good cowboy, though, I realize now, not too honest."

"What are you going to do?"

He looked at me amused. "I'll sleep on it, I'm tired."

"But…"

"You better get some sleep too." He brushed his thumb over my lower lip in an almost imperceptible caress that sent a shiver down my spine. I immediately turned my head away.

"Aren't you going to...?"

"To sleep, Aisha."

Apparently, that was all the thanks I would get. Indignant, I straightened up to leave the office, but his voice stopped me before I reached the door.

"Aisha…"

I turned with my chin in the air.

"I owe you one, princess."

I rolled my eyes and slammed the door on my way out.

9

Spring finally took hold. Temperatures rose slowly but surely, and the snow began to melt rapidly. A few flowers tentatively poked their heads out, and the cows' calvings became more and more spaced out, until one day Al announced that calving was over.

Since they learned that I had helped bring a calf into the world, the cowboys looked at me differently. Suddenly, I was one of them, though my ignorance of such matters remained much the same. I had long ago given up my plan to be as obnoxious as possible. Almost without realizing it, I had stopped trying to get kicked off the ranch. In fact, I had resigned myself to spending the rest of my 'sentence' in the Double B.

I hadn't confessed it to anyone, but the wide open spaces and towering mass of the snow-capped Teton Range fascinated me more and more every day. If someone had told me that a die-hard urbanite like myself, who had moved from a big city like Chicago to an even bigger one like Los Angeles, would suddenly develop a passion for wide open, semi-wild spaces, I would have laughed in their face. And of course, I didn't even want to think about the sudden crazy love I had for Maleficent and Maya, two animals that would have given me the heebie-jeebies just a few months earlier.

I hardly recognized myself. I was beginning to build a genuine friendship with Zoe and Carol; even the exchanges between Fernanda and me were often almost friendly. If it weren't for the fact that I still found Vance's stepmother unbearable, I would have begun to worry deeply.

I had even agreed to help the students at Wilson's school with the end-of-year party. Linda, the principal, and I had hit it off the moment we met, and I had been driving to the small town three afternoons a week ever since. She had even offered me a modest salary to help pay off my debts.

I had never worked with children before. In fact, I had never interacted with them at all, and it was a real eye-opener. Linda often insisted that I should stay and live there to teach ballet and modern dance to the village children who had so few opportunities to do anything but help on their parents' farms. I just laughed at this crazy idea and reminded her that I wanted to get back to my life as soon as possible, although as I sat in the solitude of my room contemplating the life I should so urgently resume, it was not at all clear to me.

Despite my new job, I still helped out in the stables and rode with Vance every afternoon. Truth was, I was proud of my skills in the saddle. Even the tough-as-nails cowboy, who liked to scold me for every little thing – like galloping to death over rocky ground or trying to imitate the way the ranch cowboys got off their horses before pulling up – had to grudgingly admit that I wasn't entirely bad at it.

Between my early morning ballet routines and riding Maya in the evenings, my leg was getting stronger by the day and hardly hurt at all except when I was really tired.

The only serious setback during this almost idyllic period occurred the day Vance fired Colin and another devious-eyed cowboy who was his shadow.

One evening, barely a week after I told Vance what I had uncovered, we were gathered in the living room after dinner as usual when we began to hear angry voices. Immediately, Carol, Josh, and I jumped up and ran to the office.

"You can't fire me like this!" Colin's angry voice came through the closed door.

"Be thankful I don't bring in the sheriff." As usual, Vance remained calm. "You're lucky we're distant relatives."

"At least let me stay while I look for something else." More than a request, it sounded like an order.

"No way. I want you and your sidekick to pack your things tonight and be gone by dawn. I don't want to see either of you here again."

"This won't stand! I swear you'll pay for this!"

We heard a clatter, as if someone had thrown a chair on the floor, and the three of us looked at each other, not quite knowing what to do.

"Don't be an idiot, Colin. Don't make it harder."

Just then, the door burst open and Vance, who had a firm grip on the cowboy's shoulder, shoved him roughly out of the office.

Colin staggered, but managed to regain his balance. Then he noticed our presence and, realizing that we had witnessed his humiliation, lashed out at me with hateful eyes. "Bitch! You think I don't know it was you who spilled the beans?"

I froze, but before I had time to react, Josh stepped between us and Vance was restraining Colin with a Nelson wrench.

"If you insult or threaten her again, I swear your buddy will have to scoop up what's left of you with a teaspoon." Although Vance didn't raise his voice, his tone made me hold my breath. Without letting go, he dragged Colin to the front door and threw him out.

"You will pay for this!" We heard him yell one more time before Vance slammed the door shut.

Josh confronted his big brother. "Are you just going to let him walk away like it's no big deal? You should have called the cops, you know very well that cattle rustling is considered a very ugly crime in this state."

"Let it be, Josh. I didn't do it for him, I did it for his mother. But if he ever bothers anyone on this ranch again, I'll show no mercy."

His eyes were on me. I knew he was deadly serious, and, I don't know why, I got the impression he was mad at me, too.

"Come on, let's go in the living room and I'll fix you a drink." Carol, who was an expert at defusing tense situations, stepped in at the right moment.

"I don't like alcohol very much, thank you. I'm going to bed. Good night."

Vance didn't even answer, and that made me mad. I couldn't understand why he was angry with me.

"See what happens when you stick your nose where it doesn't belong?" I scolded myself on the way to my bedroom. "Next time don't get smart; you definitely look prettier when you keep your mouth shut."

I went straight to bed and promptly fell asleep. When I woke up, the alarm had not yet gone off. Rays of pink light drew me to the window and I held my breath at the beauty of the sunrise.

I quickly slipped my bare feet into my boots, covered myself with the fur blanket and stepped out onto the balcony. The freshness of the clean air hit my face. I inhaled the scent of the pine trees and snuggled up more tightly into the blanket. In front of me, a vast meadow, dotted with small patches of snow, stretched up to the foothills of the mountains, tinted a deep blue that contrasted with the pinkish hue of the peaks. A few low, vaporous-looking clouds gave the landscape a fairytale feel.

I took another deep breath.

"I'm going to miss all of this when I get back to Los Angeles," I said to myself, feeling the longing once again for something I couldn't name.

I heard a noise behind me and turned quickly. Despite the cold, Vance was dressed in jeans and no covering other than one of his usual flannel shirts and, of course, the Stetson. Without a word, he stood beside me, resting his forearms on the wooden railing and admiring the spectacular panorama.

I didn't say anything either. In fact, I was still mad at him. We stood in silence for a long time, watching the pink clarity give way to a golden light that dissipated the shadows in its wake.

"I want you to stay away from Wilson for a few days."

Absorbed as I was in that magical play of light, I had almost forgotten his presence, and I started at the sound of his voice. "What do you mean?"

"I don't want you to go out there alone."

"You don't really think Colin's dangerous." My voice was laced with disdain.

"Sometimes people surprise you," he said calmly, not taking his eyes off the mountains.

"Bah. That's ridiculous, Vance. Besides, even if he is, am I going to be cooped up on the ranch for the rest of my life?

"Just for a few days. I'll talk Tom into inviting him to leave Wyoming."

He said it so matter-of-factly that I had no doubt that Tom, the sheriff, would do exactly what the owner of the Double B asked. However, it was time for him to understand that I was not one of his pawns to be moved at his whim. "I'm sorry, but no. I'm going to live my life the way I always have. I can't break my commitments every time some idiot makes a few threats."

Finally, he turned around. He leaned his hips against the railing, crossed his ankles, hooked his thumbs into the thick leather belt with the silver buckle – as ever-present as his hat – and fixed his eyes on me. The man's poses were right up there with those of the cowboy in the Marlboro ad, I thought with annoyance. The only thing missing was the cigarette hanging from his lips.

"Please?"

Shit, how could this man know me so well? I had never been able to resist doing things when asked nicely; what I couldn't stand was being ordered around.

Frowning, I considered my answer for a few seconds. "Okay, but just for this week."

"Just for this week."

He took a step toward me. He gently closed the ends of the blanket, which had slipped a little, around my neck, and the light touch of his long fingers on the sensitive skin of my throat took my breath away.

"Thank you." The corners of his eyes crinkled in his characteristic seductive gesture, but before I could turn purple from lack of oxygen, he turned away and went back to his room.

I shook my head in disgust. I didn't understand why I ran out of breath every time that cowboy touched me. He wasn't even my type. Anyway… I shrugged, went back to my room and got ready to go downstairs for breakfast.

In the end, staying at the ranch turned out not to be such a terrible punishment. The sun was shining brightly those days, and as soon as we finished our chores, Zoe, Carol, and I would go for a ride.

At the beginning of my stay at the ranch, Zoe couldn't stand me. Every time she saw me with Vance, she would make a face, and her every comment was peppered with jealousy. But in the last few weeks, her attitude toward me had completely changed, and I suspected that Brad, the blond cowboy with the long ponytail, had a lot to do with it. Since I'd been helping her with the books, she and Brad had been spending more time together, and it didn't take a genius to figure out that the teenage crush Zoe had on Vance was turning into something much deeper, just with another man. I liked that state of affairs; I guess because Zoe and I were starting to become good friends.

"It would be great if we went to Wilson's on Saturday. There's a well-known country band playing at the Coach."

Carol's enthusiasm was contagious and we immediately began making plans. I hadn't been out at night since I arrived in Wyoming and was curious about the local nightlife, if there was any.

"We have to get the guys to come," Zoe said.

"At least Brad, right?" I grinned mischievously.

Carol and I burst out laughing when she blushed, but Zoe countered right away, "And Vance, of course."

"And Vance too, of course." Now it was Carol's turn to grin mischievously.

"I hope you're not saying that because of me," I put on the same face a tolerant adult would put on in response to the nonsense of a couple of impertinent girls, "because I have to tell you, if you are, you're very much mistaken."

Carol and Zoe exchanged a knowing look, but I decided not to take it personally. I looked around and suddenly stood up on my stirrups and pointed in the direction of the river. A few yards away from a grove of birch trees, there was a mound that caught my attention. "What's that?"

"What is it?" Zoe and Carol looked in the same direction.

"I think it's a wounded animal."

Without waiting for them, I spurred Maya on and headed in that direction at full speed. When I reached the mound, I leapt from my horse. It was indeed a cow, but it wasn't injured, it was dead. Zoe and Carol arrived just then and also dismounted to examine my find.

"She's been shot, no doubt about it." Zoe pointed to the ominous hole under the animal's jaw and shook her head pessimistically. "Boy, Vance is going to be pissed."

As if he knew we were talking about him, I looked up just then and saw three cowboys approaching at a gallop. I took off my hat and frantically waved it over my head. Immediately, the lead rider pulled on the reins and forced his mount to turn in our direction, while the other two followed close behind.

"What's it?" Vance was the first to dismount.

Zoe pointed to the carcass. "She's been shot."

Josh and Miguel approached the corpse with a grim look on their faces.

"It's fresh, the scavengers barely nibbled at it," the latter said.

"It's been a long time since we had a problem with rustlers." Josh kicked a nearby rock angrily.

"They're not rustlers, not even poachers." Nothing in Vance's face betrayed his thoughts.

"No?" Carol said, her eyes wide.

Zoe and I looked at Vance inquisitively.

"They didn't take the cow alive, did they? They didn't take the meat, did they?" It seemed Miguel was as testy as his wife.

"Colin?" Josh didn't take his eyes off his brother.

"I talked to Tom. He went to his mother's house, but she didn't know anything. Apparently there's no trace of him or his sidekick."

"Maybe he's gone somewhere else," I said hopefully.

The three men turned and looked at me pitifully, making me feel like a hopeless optimist.

"We need to step up our surveillance," Vance finally said. "We may need to hire more men. Josh, send someone to bury the remains."

Without further ado, Vance jumped on his horse and galloped away.

The sheriff, who had stopped by the ranch at Vance's request, also ruled out rustlers, although he said theft had increased in recent months because of high beef prices. A prolonged drought had reduced cattle numbers, but global demand for beef continued to rise. In addition, Black Angus beef was the most popular meat in the United States, so no one would miss the opportunity to take more than a thousand pounds, which could be worth several thousand dollars on the black market.

After the commotion caused by the discovery of the dead cow, it took a few days for things to get back to normal, but Saturday finally came and we, the Double B girls, got ready for our night out.

It had been ages since I had dressed up. I hadn't worn skirts or dresses since the accident, but I had traded in my usual jeans and flannel shirt for tight black pants and a fine wool v-neck sweater in a light shade that really suited me. I had also put on makeup for the first time in months. I looked at my reflection in the mirror and told myself with satisfaction that I might not be the belle of the ball, but I was certainly not going to be a wallflower.

We had agreed to meet in the foyer, and when I went downstairs I was surprised to see Josh and Vance standing next to Zoe and Carol, looking very smart in their dark jeans and white shirts, their damp hair neatly combed.

"Are you guys coming?"

"We're not going to let the three most beautiful women in town go without a proper escort, are we, brother?" Vance looked me up and down and shook his head silently. "There's a lot of smooth talkers loose in Wilson. Let's go, fair ladies." Josh gallantly stepped aside for us to pass.

We girls, squeezed into the back of one of the ranch's pickup trucks, talking and laughing all the way. Truth was, I hadn't felt such anticipation since I went to my high school prom with the hottest guy in the class.

There were already a lot of cars parked on the esplanade in front of the Stagecoach Bar, so the night promised to be lively. Brad was waiting for us at the door. As soon as we got out of the truck he rushed over to greet us. He, too, had put on his best clothes and pulled his hair back in a long blond braid. The look of absolute mutual admiration that he and Zoe exchanged was quite comical.

The next encounter, however, was not so pleasant. As soon as I entered the place, the first thing I saw was Colin and his buddy at the bar, drinking beer and chatting with some women.

Vance immediately approached them, and although I could not hear his words from where I was and over all the noise, it was not hard to guess from the look of the owner of the Double B and the defiant expression on his interlocutor's face that the conversation was not going very well.

When he rejoined us, he said something to his brother, who nodded in agreement. Vance caught me looking at him and must have noticed my concern because he immediately approached me. "Ignore him."

"What did you say to him?"

"I told him the sheriff was looking for him and wanted to ask some questions about one of my cows that had been shot. He said he didn't know what I was talking about, that he had come to Wilson to have a good time, but that he had no intention of sticking around. He said he's been offered a good job in Utah."

"Do you believe him?"

Vance shrugged. "Whether I do or not, I have no proof that he's the one who killed the cow, and I don't feel like calling Tom and ruining everyone's evening."

I bit my lip in concern. I didn't trust Colin in the least, but I didn't think he'd dare do anything crazy in front of so many witnesses. As usual, Vance read my mind.

"Relax, there are too many people here for him to try one of those little stunts he likes so much."

I nodded, though I wasn't too convinced.

"Our table is ready," Josh said at that moment.

We sat down at one of the tables near the dance floor and ordered drinks and snacks. It was still a while before the show started. Everyone there seemed to know everyone else, and I lost count of how many people came up to the table to say hello. Soon I had forgotten all about Colin.

As soon as we finished eating, the band started to play. I had never been a big fan of country music, but I got into the groove right away. The waiter had just removed my empty plate when a man I had been introduced to, but whose name I had already forgotten, asked me to dance.

"I have no idea how to dance this."

"Don't worry about it, Aisha," said Josh, who was already getting up to ask a pretty brunette he had greeted enthusiastically when he arrived for a dance. "The two-step is an easy dance, you'll get the hang of it in no time."

I glanced hesitantly at Vance, who was talking to an acquaintance. He sensed my apprehension and said with a smile, "You'll do just fine, princess."

The truth was, it didn't seem too complicated, and my legs tingled with the desire to dance. So I stood up and accepted the cowboy's arm with a smile.

I immediately understood the dynamics of the dance. It was simple, really: two fast and two slow steps, repeated over and over, while my partner, with his left hand intertwined with mine and the other at shoulder blade level, led me around the dance floor.

I danced and danced until the faces of my successive partners blurred in my mind. I was very aware, however, that there was someone I hadn't danced with yet. My leg began to bother me, but I ignored the ache; I was having too much fun.

The last notes of a lively melody had just died away when I felt a tap on my shoulder. I turned with a smile, ready to dance with the next person who asked, and was surprised to see Vance behind me. I'd been watching him out of the corner of my eye, and although I'd seen him talking to several very pretty women, he hadn't danced with any of them. So I concluded that dancing was not his thing.

"Do you want to dance?" I asked doubtfully.

"Of course I do."

He held me in that somewhat impersonal way that was the norm, but, I don't know why, this time it seemed different. The distance between our bodies was considerable, but through our intertwined hands and the one on his shoulder, I could feel the intense heat he gave off.

"You dance very well," he said as he expertly spun me around.

"You sure can dance well."

"You look surprised."

"I hadn't seen you dance all night, so I thought you didn't know how."

"On the contrary, I love it. Unfortunately, I don't practice much." He spun me around again and made an elaborate arm movement that I easily imitated. He smiled at me, his masculinity more pronounced than ever. "I've never danced with a woman who followed me so easily."

"It's not my merit. I just hear the rhythm of a song and my body begins to move on its own."

"Now pay attention." I let myself go without the slightest resistance. He was so strong and paced so skillfully that he made me feel almost immaterial.

The sound of applause and high-pitched whistles made me turn my head to see that a circle had formed around us. I felt my cheeks light up, and the curious smile on my partner's firm lips made me blush even more. Luckily, the song ended just then.

"We have to do it again, Aisha."

"Yes, of… of course." For some strange reason, I was suddenly dead embarrassed and my eyes were everywhere but on him.

"Well, there is no better time than the present." Before I knew it, he had me in his arms again, this time holding me tightly. Then I noticed that someone had dimmed the lights and the first chords of a slow song were playing.

"It's called *I Cross My Heart* by George Strait," Vance whispered so close to my ear that I shivered. "It's one of my favorites."

The romantic lyrics, his closeness, and the scent of his skin made me dizzy. My heart was beating too fast for such a slow rhythm. I rested my palms against his chest and, summoning all my willpower, I pushed him away a little and looked into his eyes.

"Vance…"

"Yes, Aisha?"

I cleared my throat nervously and said sharply, "I don't know exactly what you're looking for, but I can't give it to you."

"Eric?"

"Eric and… everything."

"What is it *exactly*," he emphasized the word, "that you think I'm looking for?"

I saw the familiar wrinkles at the corners of his eyes and realized that not only was he not the least bit offended by my words, but that he was having a great time at my expense.

When I realized that he was making fun of something that seemed very serious to me, I got cross, but tried to speak calmly. "I think you're looking for an uncomplicated affair. The ranch is pretty isolated, and with so much work you don't have time to go to Jackson or Wilson to hang out with girls. So what I'm *exactly* thinking," I emphasized the word just as he had, "is that having me around suits you, especially since you know I'll be out of your life in no time."

"Would you prefer a more serious relationship?"

I hastened to shake my head in annoyance. "Of course not! I don't deny that an uncomplicated affair might have some appeal, but I'm not even ready for something like that."

"I see."

"So?"

"Let's dance, and later we'll talk about what kind of relationship we want."

"There won't be…"

Without letting me finish the sentence, he put a hand behind my head and pressed it to his chest. "Shut up and dance."

I surprised myself by obeying such an unsubtle command. With a sigh, I closed my eyes and lost myself in the beauty of the melody, the comforting warmth of the arms around me, and the scent of the mixture of soap, leather, and the outdoors that was so much his. Shortly after, the song ended, and almost immediately a much more upbeat one began.

"No, I'm sorry, I'm exhausted. I'm going to sit down for a while," I said to Mike, a cowboy I'd danced with twice before and who had rushed over as soon as he saw Vance let go of me.

I dropped into the chair, not only physically exhausted, and took a long swig of my beer. It was lukewarm and didn't taste very good, but at least it quenched my thirst after all that exercise.

I looked for Carol and Zoe among the couples crowding the place. I immediately spotted Vance's sister dancing with a boy with a severe acne problem who didn't look much older than her and who was awkwardly leading her around. Zoe and Brad, on the other hand, were experts at the two-step, moving deftly up and down the dance floor.

I covertly stretched out my leg – the exertion was taking its toll – and glanced sideways at the corner where Vance and a stunning blonde with the look of a rodeo queen were chatting animatedly. I felt a twinge of something unpleasant and looked away immediately; I had no desire to delve into the meaning of this sensation.

After a while I yawned and blinked a few times; I had suddenly become very sleepy. I raised my glass to my mouth in an attempt to clear my head, but it slipped through my fingers and crashed to the floor, splattering everything with a shower of beer and glass. Unable to move, I stared in amazement at the little mess.

"What is it, Aisha?"

Stunned, I lifted my eyes to Vance who had rushed over, but I couldn't focus.

"Vance…" I tried to say something, but I could not force my throat muscles to obey and I felt my eyelids close again.

"Aisha." Someone slapped my face to wake me up. "Aisha!"

I was unable to answer or open my eyes. Little by little I was sinking into a pit of deep physical discomfort and there was nothing I could do about it. I had the same feeling as the day I took codeine again to ease the pain and I was on the verge of dying.

This thought woke me up a little. Terrified, I tried to hold on to Vance's arm, but my fingers wouldn't obey either. I made a superhuman effort and managed to get a word out, "Drugs…"

"Drugs, have you been doing drugs?" I could barely shake my head.

"Mike, do you have anything in the ambulance to give her an emergency stomach pump?"

Even though I couldn't move or speak, I could register what was going on around me, and at Vance's words I remembered that this Mike guy had told me he was a paramedic and that he drove Wilson's only ambulance. I didn't hear what Mike said, but I noticed that I was being picked up and taken to another place where the noise of people and music was faint.

"You better get out of here, this is not going to be pleasant. I will have to insert a tube and aspirate the stomach contents, I may even be forced to use activated charcoal."

"I want to stay."

"Do as I say, Vance, and don't worry, it's not the first time I've done this."

I heard a door close and, for the second time in my life, I was subjected to a gastric lavage. As soon as I felt the tip of the probe in one of my nostrils, I tried to fight. It was useless, my body did not respond to the commands of my brain, so I was forced to endure the unpleasant process without resistance.

A long time later I heard a knock at the door and I opened my eyes exhausted.

"Come in, we're done."

Vance entered the small room that must have been someone's office. "How is she?"

"She's out of danger, but I'm taking her to the hospital for at least one night of observation."

When I heard this, I tried to sit up. "No! Not to the hospital."

Vance took my hand and tried to reassure me. "It will only be for one night, I promise. To make sure you're okay."

Tears began to slide down my cheeks, uncontrollably. "Please, Vance," I begged, "don't do this. They'll say it was a relapse. They'll put me in a mental institution. Please!"

I think it was my state of nervous excitement that made him reconsider the situation. He looked at Mike very seriously. "What if I take her to the Double B?"

"Nothing should happen, but I can't assure you that things will go smoothly. It would be a good idea to have someone watch her tonight."

His green eyes were on me again, his lips tight, but he finally nodded his head as if he had just made up his mind. "Okay. I'll take care of her tonight."

Unable to put into words the relief I felt, all I could do was give him a faint smile, which was suddenly wiped away when I saw the condition the owner of the Double B was in that I hadn't noticed before. "What happened?"

He had a bruise on his cheekbone and a small cut on his lip that was bleeding a little, and several buttons were missing from his shirt.

"Nothing to worry about."

I looked down at his hands and saw that his knuckles were raw.

"Did you get into a fight?" I frowned in confusion. I was still quite dizzy and it took me a while to realize what must have happened. "You had a fight with Colin." This time it was a confirmation.

"Look, princess, it's late. I'll tell you all about it some other time. We're going home now. You need to rest."

"But just tell me..."

"Another time." He took my jacket that someone had brought, helped me put it on, and buttoned it up to my chin.

"It's not fair, Vance, I won't be able to sleep a wink unless you tell me..."

Without heeding me, he took me in his arms again.

"I owe you big time," he said to Mike.

"Don't worry, I'll get even. I saw one of your promising colts the other day," he replied with a wink.

"Thanks Mike, I don't know what would have happened to me without your help." I gave him a weak smile. Despite my best efforts, my eyelids insisted on closing.

"Just send me an invitation."

"An invitation?" I repeated, puzzled, but Vance was already striding away and no one answered me. "What do you think he meant?"

"Not the slightest." He shook his head, very seriously.

10

I remember little else about that night, except that when I opened my eyes, the midday light was streaming into my bedroom. My head ached and my tongue was fuzzy, but I still felt a deep sense of well-being. Blinded by the sun's rays, I closed my eyelids again in a desperate attempt to catch the elusive trace of a dream.

I couldn't remember ever having such an erotic dream. I shuddered. I still seemed to feel the strong arms of a naked man around my body; the searing heat given off by the muscular chest on which I had rested my cheek; the desire, like liquid lava, that the contact of lips on mine and along my neck had ignited between my legs; the delicacy of a fiery hand tracing the curve of my hips… I felt my cheeks flush. My breathing was ragged and I was highly aroused, but then rather confused images of what had happened the night before flooded in and instantly destroyed my well-being.

Drugs. Someone had slipped a drug into my drink. I slammed my fist down hard on the pillow. Had I been in front of that 'someone,' I would have beaten him viciously. Colin. Of course, I understood everything now. The dream had been nothing more than a hallucination caused by whatever it was I had been given. The anger I felt made me open my eyes and I discovered Carol sitting in an armchair that she had moved closer to the bed, reading a book.

"Carol…" Saying that one word scratched my sore throat.

Although I had spoken very quietly, the teenager looked up immediately. "Finally you wake up, Sleeping Beauty."

I tried to sit up, but I felt a strange heaviness in my limbs.

"Wait, I'll help you!" Carol jumped out of the chair, put another pillow on my back, and helped me lie back against the headboard. The sheets slid down to my hips and I realized I was wearing only my panties and bra. I hurried to cover up and forced myself to ask a question I didn't want to ask, "Did you undress me?"

I crossed my fingers and prayed for a 'yes,' but she flatly denied it. "No, I didn't. It was Vance who took you to the bedroom."

I felt a surge of fire rise in my cheeks and when she saw it, Carol winked at me mischievously. "Don't worry, my big brother is very discreet."

"He could have asked Fernanda," I said grumpily. I hated the idea that the cowboy had seen the scars on my leg.

"Don't think about it."

Yeah, right, like it was that easy. Suddenly, I had a disturbing thought.

"Have you been here long?" I was reluctant to ask certain questions, but somehow I felt compelled.

"Since about seven thirty or so. Today will not be an easy day for Vance and he had no choice but to leave early. He ordered me to take good care of you.

I wasn't amused by the playful smile on her face, but even though my alarm was growing by the minute, I decided it would be better to change the subject. "Do you know what happened while Mike was looking after me? Vance and Colin got into a fight, didn't they?"

"You wouldn't believe it!" Carol looked like she was going to burst with excitement. "You turned all white and Mike and my brother dragged you into the manager's office and slammed the door in our faces. Josh, Zoe, Brad and I were waiting on the other side, and you should have seen Vance when he finally came out! He had the word 'murder' written all over his face. I promise you, even I was scared.

I had no trouble believing it. Ever since I met him, I had suspected that the day the cowboy lost control would be terrifying.

"And?" I asked impatiently.

"We went back to the main room and he was told that Colin and his sidekick had just left. When he heard that, Vance took off and we followed him at a run to the parking lot. Colin tried to close the door of his truck, but

Vance yanked him out and threw him to the ground. Then Colin yelled at him what the 'ahem, ahem' – she raised her eyebrows in a very expressive way – he was doing, and my brother yelled back what the 'ahem, ahem' he put in your drink. And that's when Colin really screwed up…

She fell silent, although it was obvious that she was desperate to continue the story. However, the little torturer obviously wanted me to beg her to continue. So I begged, "Please continue. How did he screw up?"

"He got cocky and, boy, was that a big mistake. You know what he said?"

I shook my head impatiently. "How could I? At that moment I was locked in a room, undergoing an unpleasant process of pipes cleaning."

"Colin said, 'Are you going to believe what a junkie says?'"

"Son of a bitch!" I couldn't help it, but Carol, always so polite in her speech, wasn't the least bit shocked.

"Precisely. It was his death sentence."

"What?!" I almost screamed.

"Figuratively speaking, of course. That is, if Brad and Josh hadn't held him back, I have no doubt that would have been the outcome. Vance punched him until his face was a pulp. I'm afraid Colin won't be doing much flirting for a while. As he groaned on the parking lot floor, Vance began rifling through his pockets until he found some Ro-hyp-nol pills." She spelled the name slowly to make sure she had it right. "Then he threw them at him with all his might, aiming so well that some hit him in the one eye that wasn't half closed from the blows."

"I hope Vance doesn't have a problem with the sheriff."

"With Tom? No way," Carol dismissed the idea with a wave of her hand. "There are plenty of witnesses to the fact that it was a clean fight. In fact, Colin was lucky that his buddy loaded him into the truck and took him away before Tom got there. Now there's an APB out on him, so if he shows up here again, he'll end up in the slammer."

I wasn't too reassured by this news. From what little I had seen of Colin, I knew he was a vindictive bastard and I didn't like the idea of him being on the loose. He could hurt Vance.

Just then there was a knock at the door and Carol opened it to make room for Fernanda, who was carrying a tray of food.

"Room service for the *señoritinga*. Someone must think this is a hotel." Her sarcasm cheered me up. After the dark events of the night before, Fernanda's attitude was a welcome return to normalcy.

"That's nice of that 'someone,' but you didn't have to go to any trouble." I gave her an angelic smile and turned to Carol as if the other wasn't there. "I gotta tell you, that woman can surprise me sometimes."

With a snort, Fernanda placed the tray on my thighs, and between the smell of the latte and the freshly baked scones, my mouth watered.

"Thanks, they look great." I smiled warmly at her, and sensing my sincerity, the tiny woman seemed to soften.

"I'll bring you something more substantial for dinner."

My mouth was full, so I shook my head.

"No need, really," I said when I managed to swallow. "As soon as I'm done with this, I'm going to take a shower and get back to my normal life."

Fernanda looked at me disapprovingly. "Vance is not going to like that."

"And why does everyone think I should care what that cowboy likes or dislikes?" I replied with my usual defiance.

Now it was her turn to give me an angelic smile. "I remind you, *señoritinga*, that he's the one who gives the orders around here."

"Well, not to me!"

"Todavía no te has dado cuenta de que te ha marcado con su hierro como a una becerra? (*Haven't you noticed yet that he has branded you with his iron like a calf?)" she said in Spanish.

"Would you mind speaking in plain English? I don't understand this gibberish."

"One day you will" I didn't like the way she looked at me, as if she knew something I, poor fool, didn't. "Anyway, I'd better go, I have much more important things to do."

As soon as she left, I asked Carol, "You understand Spanish, what did she say?"

"I don't know, she spoke too fast," she said. The innocent look on her face told me she understood well enough.

When she saw me open my mouth to insist, Carol looked at her watch with an exaggerated gesture. "Oh, it's so late! I have to go too. Goodbye. If you need me, just shout!"

And before I could stop her, she was gone.

Sulking, I ate down to the last crumb, but by the time I put the tray away, I felt much better. Food had restored my strength. I carefully stood up and, seeing that I wasn't dizzy, went to the bathroom. The hot shower cleared my head and after washing my hair and brushing my teeth, I felt completely recovered. I put on my usual clothes: jeans, boots and a thick sweater and went downstairs.

The house was quiet. I figured Tessa would be in Jackson as usual and the rest would be working somewhere in the Double B, so I went to the office hoping to find Zoe, but there was no one there either.

There was a pile of papers on the desk and I decided it would be a good idea to try and organize the mess a bit. The sun was streaming through the uncurtained window and the warm atmosphere was comforting. Absorbed in my task of sorting and classifying, I forgot the passage of time until the door opened and the owner of the Double B himself entered the office.

I looked away from the screen and, unable to help myself, my eyes took a tour of their own. The mud-stained leather boots, the worn jeans that emphasized the length of the powerful legs, the plaid shirt with the last two buttons undone showing the tanned skin… and when they finally stopped on his face, the amusement I read in those striking golden-green irises made me turn beet red. Slowly, he pulled back his hat in his usual manner, and I noticed my mouth going dry.

"Enjoying the view?" His mocking comment snapped me out of this sort of drooling-dog contemplation.

"What view? I was just surprised to see you here at this hour."

"It's nearly dinnertime."

He rounded the desk and sat on the edge, and I had to push my chair back a little to keep his thigh from brushing my arm.

"Already?" I looked out the window and saw that the sun was setting. I hadn't realized it was so late.

"Why aren't you in bed?"

I raised my chin defiantly. "I'm fine, I don't need to stay in bed."

"I told Fernanda I wanted you to rest."

"Too bad. You know I don't take orders from anyone."

"Hum."

"Hum, what?"

Without answering, he cupped my chin gently and studied me carefully. My cheeks felt hot again, but then I noticed the cut on his lip and the bruise on his cheekbone and immediately pushed aside the pleasant sensation of his long fingers touching my skin. I reached up and barely brushed the pad of my thumb against his injured lip.

"I'm sorry."

"Don't be."

Unable to face the strange glint in his eyes, I dropped my hand and looked down.

"It was very unpleasant, and on top of that, you were forced to fight. Carol told me everything." I cleared my throat sheepishly. "I'm sorry to have caused you so much trouble, maybe it's time for me to go home."

"Home?" he said quietly.

A simple question that reminded me that I no longer had a home. Sure, the ramshackle apartment I had rented after leaving the one I shared with Eric was not my home. In fact, maybe I should rethink the idea of moving back to Los Angeles; there was no point in going back there. Maybe I could go to Chicago or… Definitely, the cowboy must have had mind reading superpowers, because he instantly guessed the direction of my thoughts.

"It's better if you stay a few more months and figure out what you want to do with your life in the meantime."

"I could visit Raff in Madrid. A trip might help me clear up my ideas."

"Raff just got married. You don't want to interrupt the two lovebirds on their honeymoon."

I bit my lip. No, I had no desire to share my brother with his new wife. I might not even like her. The truth was, I didn't want to think about Raff's marriage right now, so I abruptly changed the subject. "Were you… ?" I stopped, cleared my throat, and started again, feeling myself blush some more. Being so pale was a drag. "Were you the one who undressed me last night?"

"You mean when you were half unconscious and I took you to your bedroom?"

I narrowed my eyes. "You know what, Vance Bennet? You remind me of my brother more and more every day, and I don't mean that as a compliment."

"Your brother? No way. I'm nothing like your brother, forget it."

The way he said it, so bluntly, annoyed me. "There's no need to get unpleasant."

"I mean," he gave me one of those beatific smiles, identical to the ones Raff used when he wanted to play innocent, "that when I'm by your side, my feelings are not at all... brotherly."

I blinked a few times. Was he hitting on me? Of course he was hitting on me, I wasn't stupid enough not to notice. Was it because of last night? After all, he had seen me half naked. I put my hands to my cheeks, which were burning again. "Did you see... ? Did you see me... ?"

"Despite my thirty percent Sioux blood, I am a gentleman." He went off on a tangent, but the wrinkles at the corners of his eyes told me all I needed to know.

"So you've seen my scars."

Vance regained his seriousness on the spot. "The only thing I saw last night was that you have a knockout body."

I squeezed my eyelids shut for a few seconds, wondering if a person could die of embarrassment, but I got over it and said sternly, "I don't like being undressed when I'm unconscious."

Vance pulled his hat back an inch. "Don't worry, Aisha, I promise you, the next time I undress you, you will be in full possession of your mental faculties."

That was not what I wanted to hear and even less with the tone he used, as if we both knew that undressing me again was only a matter of time. The truth was that I didn't like the direction our conversation had taken; however, I still had one more question to ask. The question that had been haunting me since I opened my eyes a few hours ago.

"It wasn't a dream, was it?" I whispered, my eyes locked with his.

I didn't have to explain what I was talking about. Vance shook his head without saying anything.

"You took advantage of me," I said quietly.

Again he just nodded.

"That's… that's not very gentlemanly of you."

"Blame it on my hot Mexican blood."

"It's not funny, Vance."

"No, you're right, it's not funny."

He put his palms on my shoulders and fixed his eyes on mine.

"I was really worried about you last night. I promised Mike I'd keep an eye on you, remember?" I nodded silently.

"You were so restless, moaning like you were having a terrible nightmare. I told myself that maybe if I hugged you you would calm down, but I didn't expect you to react like this…"

Those enigmatic words made me feel very uncomfortable, but I wanted to get to the bottom of this thorny matter right away. "React how?"

"You threw your arms around my neck and clung to me like a limpet. I wish I could tell you that I behaved like the gentleman we talked about earlier, but lying is not cool. The truth is, I couldn't help myself. You know, it's been a while since I've been with a woman, and you make such sexy noises when…"

"Stop it! I don't want to hear any more!"

He shut up immediately. Furious and with my cheeks burning, I shook off his hands and started pacing the office. "I find it incredible that you would blame a semi-conscious woman for your lack of self-control. Are you going to do the same thing every time you come across one in that condition?"

"Hey, this doesn't happen to me every day."

"Stop it, Vance! I can't stand it when you laugh at me!"

"But I wasn't even smiling," he protested.

"It doesn't matter. It's your eyes; the lines forming at the corners of your eyes. I don't care what you say, I know you're laughing at me, so stop it!"

Vance stepped in front of me, grabbed my arms and looked me straight in the eye, but this time he was serious, "Sorry, Aisha, you're absolutely right. I shouldn't have jumped into bed with you in the state you were in, though I swear my intentions were good. I just wanted to calm you down."

I didn't take my eyes off his face, and it seemed to me that his apology was sincere. However, there was something that kept nagging at the back of my mind.

"But you were… You were naked!" Despite the color that flooded my cheeks for the umpteenth time, I think I managed to give him an accusing look.

"If I had to choose an article of clothing to wear to bed, I'd choose the hat."

"I told you it's not funny!"

"Right. Sorry again. You see, Aisha, I've been sleeping naked since I was fourteen." He raised his eyebrows as if to apologize to me. "I swear I didn't even think about it, it was automatic."

"Well, it better not happen again. Next time…" I shut up abruptly, and yes, I noticed that I got even redder.

"I promise. Next time it will be you who undresses me."

Luckily, I didn't have to answer, because at that moment, after a light knocking, the door opened and Fernanda peeked in to announce that dinner was ready. I turned my nose up in a dignified manner and left the office, praying that my expression did not betray the arousal that had taken hold of me upon hearing his words.

11

The shock of what had happened wore off, and within a few days the residents of the Double B were back to our respective routines. I had resumed attending rehearsals at Wilson Elementary school in the afternoons, but Vance insisted that I be chaperoned at all times, and despite my protests, he was adamant. Zoe had volunteered to babysit me. One of her best friends had just given birth to her third child and had asked her to help out in the afternoons.

That day, rehearsal was not going as well as it had on other occasions. John Dylan, the male lead, announced out of the blue that he did not want to dance in the show. Apparently his older brother had caught him rehearsing the part and, not content with calling him a sissy, had assured him that he would be the laughing stock of Wilson.

You could say this was a full-blown Code Red. With only a few weeks left before the show, I didn't have time to teach the part to another kid, especially since most of the boys participating that year seemed to have two left feet.

The truth was that I was in over my head. I had no idea how I was going to pull it off. Luckily, Carla Miles, his dance partner in the number and, by the way, the most popular girl in the class – and who, I would have had no trouble believing, had just graduated with honors from a pre-teen psychology course – stepped in before I had a fit.

"Don't worry, Miss Brooks, we all know all too well what a *great* personality John Dylan has," she said sarcastically. "Besides, he's a klutz. He's been stepping on my toes the last two rehearsals."

"I'm not a klutz!" John protested angrily, his cheeks bright red.

It was clear that Carla had struck a nerve. I also suspected that the boy, like most of his classmates, had quite a crush on her and this comment, made in front of everyone, was a harsh humiliation. So I grabbed this unexpected lifeline on the fly.

"It's not true that John is a klutz, Carla, and I'm going to prove it to you." I turned to the boy, whose ears were still red at the tips, and bowed elaborately. "May I have this dance, sir? Peter, turn on the music!"

Peter obeyed immediately, and as the first notes of the lively waltz that would be the highlight of the performance began to play, I placed John's right hand on my waist and wrapped my left hand around his free hand before resting my other hand on his shoulder.

"Straight back, sir."

Without appearing to be the one calling the shots, I led the boy through the basic steps and we began to spin around the stage at full speed. John's eyes lit up like stars, and when the last chords finally faded, we stopped, smiling and breathless, and high-fived to the applause of the other kids.

Carla came running up to us. "I'm sorry I said you were clumsy, John." Her blue eyes were full of admiration. "I hope you don't listen to your idiot brother, I'd love to dance with you in the show."

John nodded without saying a word, and even though his face was flushed from the exercise, I had the feeling it was getting even redder.

Proud that I'd been able to put out this little fire, I ruffled the boy's brown hair with a light caress and looked up, smiling, to find Vance leaning back in one of the auditorium seats, his arms folded across his chest as if he didn't have a care in the world, looking more manly than ever.

My stomach did a strange pirouette at the sight of his carefree attractiveness, and annoyed by this reaction, I said dryly, "What are you doing here?"

"I came to pick you up. Zoe called to tell me she's sleeping over at her friend's house. Apparently, one of the kids has a high fever and the poor thing is overwhelmed."

"I've told you many times that I don't need a babysitter," I said with a frown.

But as usual, he was unfazed by my hostile attitude and turned to the children, who were looking at us curiously.

"Congratulations, John. Wilson's men will die of envy when they see you dance. You'll see them lining up for you to tell them your secret."

"They sure will!" The boy burst out laughing, but you could tell he was proud to be congratulated by none other than the owner of the Double B, the top-notch ranch in the area.

"All right, kids. We're done for the day." Immediately there was a great commotion and they began to pick up their things amidst shouts and laughter.

I grabbed my bag too. "Seriously, Vance, you shouldn't have bothered."

Vance put a hand on the small of my back and led me to the exit. "No bother, I wouldn't have missed this waltz for the world, although if I'm honest, I think I'm jealous of John."

"Don't be silly!" I cut him off. "I don't like this habit you have of flirting with me."

He sighed deeply with the air of a martyr, a model of patience. "Well, I hadn't put that on the list."

Now I was the one rolling my eyes. We walked silently to the parking lot and got into the pickup. Vance started it, put it in gear, and my eyes inadvertently admired the dark, sinewy forearm covered with a soft layer of dark hair that the rolled-up cuffs of his shirt revealed.

I bit my lower lip uneasily. I had never been so aware of a man's physical presence. The broad shoulders and the way his back tapered down to his hips; the seductive curve of his butt that fit the worn jeans like a glove; the long, straight legs that were not bent like other cowboys' from time spent on horseback... Vance had a way of filling the space that was suffocating.

I never had that feeling with Eric. True, the cowboy was more than a head taller and must have weighed at least twenty pounds more, but my ex's body was also muscular and full of power. Only I had never felt threatened next to him. And it wasn't that Vance was a threatening man. Not at all. It was just that he made me feel vulnerable. When I was around him, I had to fight the urge to curl up against his chest and let him protect me. An impulse that was completely ridiculous for a woman like me, who had been fending for herself since the age of sixteen.

"You're not falling in love with him, are you?"

I don't know where this thought came from, but I dismissed it out of hand. I still hadn't recovered from Eric. Besides, what could this cowboy and I have in common? Sure, there was an undeniable physical attraction. I still blushed when I remembered the dream that hadn't been a dream.

And suddenly I wondered why I was so reluctant to let myself go. Was I still loyal to Eric after what he had done to me? What was wrong with having a fling with Vance? I knew Raff wouldn't be amused if I hooked up with his friend, but I'd been of age for years and I wasn't going to start worrying about what my big brother thought at this point.

"Vance..." My lips spoke his name before my brain could stop them.

"Tell me, Aisha."

"I…" I stopped, unable to continue.

He glanced at me briefly before turning his eyes back to the road. "Did you know you turned tomato red?"

If there was one thing I hated more than blushing, it was being pointed out that I'd blushed. The heat in my cheeks increased exponentially.

"It's just…" I shook my head, not sure where to begin.

"Curiosity is killing me. A second ago, you seemed so distracted that I didn't want to bother you, but if you want, I can help you."

"Help me?" I blinked, puzzled. "Help me how?"

"To put your thoughts into words."

Such audacity immediately pulled me out of this uncomfortable state of speechlessness. "You have no idea what I'm thinking."

"No?"

"No!"

"Aisha, I've seen the way you look at me," he said calmly, not taking his eyes off the road.

"How do you… ? What do you mean?" I, on the other hand, never took my eyes off his profile.

"You want me."

"But how… how silly." I tried to make a joke out of it, but it didn't come out. I closed my mouth and after a while I hesitantly admitted, "OK… You're right, I do want you."

Well, I had already blurted it out, I said to myself, relieved. I had almost expected to be struck by lightning after such a confession. I saw the wrinkles in his eyes deepen, but he kept driving without saying anything.

"Well, what are we going to do about it?" I asked impatiently, trying to hide my nervousness.

After a long consideration he just said, "I can think of a few things."

Not even at a time like this could I get him to take me seriously.

"You're laughing at me, as usual," I accused him, annoyed.

Vance pulled the van to the side of the road and turned off the engine. Then he turned to me, grabbed my hands – which I kept wringing in my lap – and locked his piercing green eyes on mine. "No, Aisha, I'm not laughing at you, but before I say anything, I want to know what's on your mind."

"I…" I tried to pull my hands away, but he wouldn't let me. I cleared my throat, dead embarrassed, and said at full speed, "We could… we could have a short-lived affair. It would be convenient for you, and I could maybe… maybe it will help me forget about Eric."

The corners of his mouth slowly lifted into a lazy smile that took my breath away. "You see, Aisha…"

This unpromising start made me afraid of what would come next, so I beat him to the punch. "Really, you don't have to say it. You don't want me. Forget what I said, it was just…"

Without knowing how, I found myself glued to his chest. One of his big hands held my jaw, and although it was not a tight grip, it prevented me from moving.

"I want to make a few things clear," he said huskily. His mouth was so close to mine that I could feel the warmth of his breath brushing my lips. "One, yes, Aisha, I want you too. Two, one day you and I are going to end up in bed and set the sheets on fire." I swallowed, unable to look away from those sparkling green eyes that had me mesmerized. I wanted to say something, but he hadn't finished yet. "Third, if we make love, it won't be because I'm bored or because you want to forget an old boyfriend. Four…"

And that's when the jerk stopped.

"Four?" I urged him in a whisper.

"You're not ready to hear number four."

I shook my head in annoyance, I couldn't believe he was going to keep me in suspense until who knows when.

"At least you're going to kiss me, right?" I pressed my lips tightly together, but it was too late to stop the words.

His chest shook with suppressed laughter and I wanted to die, but then he leaned his mouth against mine and whispered, "Your wish is my command, princess."

And boy, did he kiss me. This cowboy was an expert kisser. Hot kisses that made you forget your own name; sensual kisses that made you think you were being kissed for the first time; intoxicating kisses that made you wish the moment would never end.

"You see, Aisha?" His husky voice made me open my eyes, though I was still so dazed that it was hard to understand what he was saying. Vance must have noticed, because he gently took one of my hands and placed it on his throbbing erection. "Never doubt how much I want you."

We stood like that for a while, looking into each other's eyes and communicating without words, until I finally withdrew my hand and sat back in my seat with my eyes straight ahead.

"I'll wait for you to tell me when it's time, but don't be too long, I won't be here much longer." I was proud of how calm my voice sounded.

"When the time comes, you'll be the first to know."

Then he changed the subject and started talking about the cattle that would be moved to summer pastures in the next few days. We chatted with seeming normalcy, and by the time we arrived at the ranch, at least I had managed to relax.

The next week was crazy. Like every year, the cattle had to be moved to the summer pastures, but first the newborn calves had to be tagged. Perched on the wooden fence of one of the corrals, I watched the process with fascination.

In fact, it was very similar to what I had seen in the western movies of my childhood. The cowboys lassoed the calves, grabbed them by the head, and laid them on their sides, holding them by putting their knees at their necks. But instead of branding them with the Double B's initials on a hot iron, they would use a special device to apply electronic identification buttons and ear tags so that each animal was registered with a number that could be read by a scanner.

I was glad that the Double B used this much more civilized technique. It would not have been pleasant to hear the squeals of pain from the calves while smelling the unpleasant odor of burning flesh.

The work was hard and the sun was beating down. Some cowboys protected themselves from the rising dust by covering their noses and mouths with colorful bandanas, but within minutes everyone was covered in dust and their shirts were soaked with sweat.

"Want to try?" Josh came smiling over to where I was with a lasso in his hand. He had taken off his bandana andthe lower part of his face looked much cleaner than the rest.

"No thanks," I smiled back, "it looks very difficult."

"It's no big deal. C'mon, I'll show you."

Despite my protests, Josh grabbed me by the waist and set me down as if I weighed nothing. He gave me instructions on how to flip the lasso over my head and stood behind me to help. The first attempt was a failure, as were the second and third. Laughing our heads off, we decided to try again.

"You'll never get the knack of it with this teacher."

Vance had approached and was watching us with his hands on his hips, smiling. His face was sweaty and dusty, and his teeth shone whiter than ever. His blue shirt had large dark stains under his armpits, and his pants were covered with a thin layer of dust. But despite his disheveled appearance, my stomach did its usual funny thing at the sight of him.

"I remind you that I was a finalist in the lassoing contest at the Jackson Rodeo," his brother protested good-naturedly.

"Get out of the way and let the professionals do their job."

"You got it tough, big brother, I've never seen anyone as clumsy with a lasso as Aisha."

"Hey," I tried to give Josh a threatening look, but I burst out laughing.

Like his brother, Vance positioned himself against my back. The warmth of his body enveloped me, cutting my amusement short. His scent of clean sweat, soap, horse and leather wafted into my head.

"Relax the arm."

I tried to concentrate on his instructions, but it was difficult with him so close. He had one arm around my waist and the other helping me swing the lasso over my head.

"All right, now choose where you want to aim." That deep voice so close to my ear made me very, very nervous.

"The calf with the white spot in the eye?" I asked hesitantly.

"Better an easier target. Do you see Miguel?" I nodded. Fernanda's husband, his back to us, was giving orders to some cowboys a few feet away.

"When I say 'now,' you let go, understand?" I nodded again, not taking my eyes off the foreman.

"One, two and... now!" I obeyed immediately and was surprised to see the lasso shoot out in a perfect oval and slide smoothly around the unsuspecting cowboy's shoulders.

"Pull!"

I pulled with all my might and poor Miguel was caught by the rope to the laughter of his men.

"It's not funny, Vance." Miguel's weathered, lean face showed utter disapproval.

"It wasn't me. It was her." The traitor pointed his thumb at me, leaving me alone in the face of danger.

"I… I'm sorry, Miguel, I never thought I'd make it," I apologized uneasily, Fernanda's husband had always struck me as a man not to be trifled with.

For a few seconds he stared at me with his Aztec idol face. I swallowed hard, but unexpectedly he winked at me. "I'm glad you made it. He," he pointed at Vance, who was having a field day with my predicament, "had a great teacher too."

Without further ado, he turned away and continued ordering the cowboys around.

Relieved, I turned to Vance and gave him a look that promised revenge.

When we returned to the ranch at dusk, I saw an unfamiliar SUV parked in the driveway. Thinking it was one of Tessa's guests, I hurried across the foyer to disappear up the stairs before he or she caught me up to my eyebrows in dust. But as soon as I set my foot on the first step, a very familiar voice stopped me in my tracks, "Aren't you going to say hello?"

Speechless, I turned to see the huge figure of my brother Raff standing in the doorway of the living room.

"Raff!" I ran to him screaming like a madwoman, threw my arms around his neck and wrapped my legs around his waist, not caring in the least if I stained his clothes.

Raff held me tight, and with my face buried in the hollow of his throat, I sucked in the familiar scent of my brother with relish. After a good while I untangled my legs and slid to the floor.

"Let me look at you." Raff looked me up and down. "Wow, sis, you look amazing," he said with satisfaction.

"The fresh air, I guess." I shrugged, not taking my eyes off his beloved face, which was strikingly highlighted by a pair of very blue eyes.

"That, and that we make her work hard."

At the sound of Vance's voice, I looked around and saw that most of the Bennet family was gathered in the foyer, looking at us curiously.

"Hello, Vance."

"What a surprise, Raff." They gave each other one of those big manly hugs filled with resounding back slaps.

"I see everything is… fine."

"More than fine."

The look my brother gave him didn't escape me, and I wondered what these two were up to.

"How's India?" Vance waved us into the living room. "I was sorry to miss the wedding, though Marcus filled me in on the details. And she had a daughter, right? I can't remember her name."

"Sol, but she's my daughter now, too. India is doing very well. She wanted to come and meet you, Aisha, but the doctor wouldn't let her fly. She is pregnant." His unmistakable expression of pride and the way his eyes lit up when he spoke of his new family took me by surprise and I was embarrassed as I felt a pang of jealousy.

Shortly after the inauguration of his company's new headquarters in Madrid, Raff called me to announce that he was marrying a widow with a daughter. The news came as a great surprise to me. Despite his good-natured teddy bear exterior, my brother had always been very successful with women, but I could not recall ever seeing him in love. According to what he told me, it was love at first sight, at least for him, because India only agreed to marry him when she realized it was the only way to escape the powerful man who was harassing her.

I was in a deep depression at the time, in and out of rehab, and I did not feel strong enough to fly to Spain to meet this woman whom I considered a rival, since I had been Raff's only family up to that point. So I apologized and told him that I would prefer to meet India when I was fully recovered.

Judging from what Raff told us that night – with that special wit of his that soon had us all in tears with laughter – his marriage, though it had not begun in the most orthodox way, was going very well indeed. You only had to hear him talk about his wife to understand that he was crazy about her.

Unfortunately, he also said that he could not stay. He had a very important meeting in New York and had no choice but to catch a plane the next day.

I hid my disappointment and decided to make the most of our time together. After dinner, the Bennets, as considerate as ever, left us alone. I sat on Raff's lap with an arm around his neck, as I had done as a child, and we talked almost until midnight. He showed me pictures of India, a beautiful brunette, and of his daughter Sol, who looked very much like her mother except for the blonde hair and blue eyes. He also showed me a picture of an older woman he called *la Tata* who, it seemed, was also an important member of the large family he had formed in record time.

After a second yawn, Raff told me to go to bed. The truth was that I was exhausted, but I didn't want to miss a second of being with him. Just then there was a knock on the door and Vance entered.

"I think it's time for you to go to bed, Aisha," he said.

I raised my eyes to the sky and begged for patience. Vance and my brother must have thought I was five years old.

"I'm a grown woman, not a child." I clarified, in case anyone had any doubts.

Vance raised his palms in a gesture of appeasement. "I'm sorry, I didn't mean to offend you. I'd like to talk to Raff for a while, if you don't mind."

The truth was, I was exhausted, so I kissed my brother on the cheek one last time and said good night.

"And you won't kiss me?" Vance said as I walked past him.

My brother's curious eyes darted from one to the other and I felt myself blush.

"That's not necessary," I said defiantly and left the room as quickly as I could without looking like I was running away.

"So that's the way the wind blows," Raff said.

"I reckon it's always blown that way." I heard their cryptic dialogue before I closed the door.

I frowned, wanting to know what the hell they were talking about, but no matter how close I pressed my ear to the door, I couldn't hear anything else. So I gave up and went to bed.

12

And there we were at last. Almost a week after Raff's return to Spain, it was time to take the cattle to the summer pastures. Pastures that most ranchers, no matter how many acres they owned, leased from the government so as not to deplete their own land.

I was torn between the excitement of the adventure and the trepidation of going camping for the first time in my life, with the obvious inconvenience of sleeping in a tent without a working toilet, in the middle of the wilderness.

I had made Zoe's head spin with my questions, but still I had filled and emptied the saddlebags a dozen times, changing one garment for another and then that other for the first, unable to make up my mind. It seemed impossible that I could fit everything I needed for an expedition of almost three days into that tiny space.

Fed up with my indecision, Carol had taken matters into her own hands. The day before we left, she stuffed the saddlebags with what she considered essential and took them to her room to keep me from taking everything out for the umpteenth time.

I awoke with a peculiar sense of anticipation. It was very early, but the day looked sunny and warm. On top of Maya, with my saddlebags, jacket and sleeping bag strapped securely to the back of my saddle, I rolled up my sleeves. Too nervous to stand still, I took from my pocket the red bandana Zoe had given me as a souvenir of my first cattle drive, tied it around my neck, and pulled my hat down to my eyebrows before turning once more to make sure the mule I was responsible for, loaded to the brim with supplies, was also tied securely to the saddle.

Carol and I were in charge of the cooking and logistics. I hoped that at least she knew what to do, because when I tried to protest that I didn't even know where to start, Fernanda silenced me with an emphatic gesture and told me to just follow the teenager's orders. Zoe, on the other hand, would help the cowboys lead the herd.

Deep down, I was glad for my role in the rear. From what I had been told, if the men were competent – and the Double B's men certainly were – the bigger the herd, the easier it was to lead. In theory, all you had to do was get behind the animals and they would take care of getting as far away from the horses and their riders as possible. But despite my friendship with Maleficent, I didn't relish the idea of riding near a few thousand skittish cows.

I expected to hear the deafening screams of the cowboys and to see them waving their hats in all directions like in the movies, but that was not the case. Surprised, I asked Carol, who explained that it was best to keep the cattle as quiet as possible. The cowboys would lead their horses through the thick of the herd so that the animals would get used to them and not mistake them for predators. It seemed that the natural instinct of cattle, especially in a semi-wild state, was to stay together, so the idea was to unleash that grouping instinct until the herd moved in unison.

The cowboys' efforts were beginning to bear fruit. The more sociable cows, the ones that usually acted as leaders, had already taken up positions at the head of the herd, and the others had begun to follow.

The animals' hooves kicked up a lot of dust, and Carol motioned for me to adjust my bandana over my nose and mouth. It was a mesmerizing sight. Soon the air was filled with mooing that almost drowned out the whistles of the cowboys as they skillfully moved around the herd, with the smell of the cattle and the fresh grass, the whinnying of the horses, and the shouts of the riders trying to move the animals forward. An impossible amalgam that violently assaulted all my senses.

I narrowed my eyes and it didn't take long to make out Vance's figure in the distance. The cowboy – who was wearing a light blue shirt that day – and his horse looked like one of those centaurs mentioned in the mythology books I had devoured as a child. The truth was that Vance stood out among the other men. Perhaps it was the self-confidence that characterized him, and how comfortable he seemed in his own skin despite his size, that made most of the glances converge on him. Or at least mine did. I didn't know why, but something about the way he moved drew me in like a magnet.

"We better get going." Carol's voice reminded me why we were here. I spurred Maya on with the heels of my boots and we set off at a brisk pace after the herd.

The Snake River, true to its name, meandered along the wide valley, and far beyond, the pointed, snow-capped peaks of the Tetons – the name the French-speaking trappers gave them, I imagine, out of a longing for women's breasts on their lonely nights – stood abruptly against the blue sky, like giant sentinels from another time.

Carol and I rode in lockstep amid chatter and laughter, each of us with our mule securely fastened to the saddle. The clean, crisp air went to my head, and I felt the same as if I'd had a few drinks. Occasionally the cowboys were forced to fetch a straggling animal, but the morning passed without much mishap. We walked ahead a little to prepare lunch and arrived at the rocky river ford where Carol had agreed with the boss that we would make our first stop.

"We will fix a cold lunch. Just some sandwiches."

I sighed with relief, I really couldn't picture myself cooking over a campfire. For one thing, I had no idea how to start one.

Carol had loaded the supplies with Fernanda and knew where everything was. She held out several packages to me and spread a small tablecloth on a flat rock by the shore.

"Now we're going to play assembly line."

Said and done; she cut the loaves in half and I stuffed them with cold pieces of chicken breast, chopped lettuce and a good squirt of mayonnaise from the jar. In a few minutes we had a nice mountain of sandwiches. And just in time, because the cowboys arrived with the herd. The animals stayed close to shore, drinking and munching on the grass that grew between the rocks, content to rest at last.

"How ya doing, girls? I could eat one of those cows raw."

Zoe took off her hat and wiped her sweaty brow with her shirt sleeve. Brad, who arrived just behind her, only lifted his a few inches. I don't know what kind of relationship these cowboys had with their hats, but it was certainly a close one.

We passed out the sandwiches and lukewarm beers as they arrived. Last up was Vance, who, after dismounting with his usual agility, took Ranger to the shore for a drink of water before tying him to the branch of a nearby bush. When he was done, he plopped down next to me and accepted the beer and sandwich I held out.

After taking a long swig of the beer – so long that I had to force myself to look away from the Adam's apple bobbing up and down in a hypnotic rhythm on his tanned throat – he let out a satisfied sigh.

"Mmm, delicious…" I noticed his eyes on my face, and it wasn't clear to me what or who he meant by that adjective; but to keep him from noticing my blush, I turned to one of the cowboys and held out another sandwich.

Carol and I didn't start eating until everyone was served. As soon as I took the first bite, I realized I was starving, and that simple sandwich and the lukewarm beer seemed like the most delicious meal I had ever had.

"Does your leg hurt?" Vance's deep voice pulled me out of my gastronomic ecstasy.

"No." I hastened to shake my head. The truth was, it did bother me a little.

"Of course, you wouldn't tell me if it hurt." Vance pushed his hat back a bit and took a huge bite of his sandwich.

The man read me like a book, which was very irritating.

"You think you know me so well." I raised my nose, but then remembered his comment about my insignificant nasal appendage and lowered it immediately.

Needless to say, there were the laugh lines next to his eyes; this cowboy didn't miss a thing. Annoyed, I turned to talk to Zoe and Brad, who were sitting close together a few feet away.

"We're going to rest for a while," Vance said as soon as the last of the sandwiches were gone.

The five cowboys who had accompanied us, Josh and Miguel, as one man, found a comfortable resting place nearby, stretched out their legs, crossed their ankles with their tapered leather boots pointed skyward, pulled their hats over their faces and began to nap. Carol finished packing and imitated them as Zoe and Brad took the opportunity to lose themselves in a nearby copse.

Suddenly, it was as if Vance and I had been left alone. I looked sideways at him and saw that his green eyes were sparkling with amusement.

"Tell me, city princess, how's the adventure going?"

"So far, so good," I replied dismissively. I had no intention of confessing that I was fascinated.

"You could use some rest."

I snorted in annoyance. "I don't like you treating me like a child."

"I need to change notebooks, I'm running out of pages to write down all the things you don't like." He shook his head in mock regret. "Come, lean against that."

He pointed to a rock to his left.

"What for?" I asked suspiciously.

Without answering, he stood up, leaned over me and lifted me into his arms. I only had time to stifle a gasp of surprise before he put me down beside the rock. Then he returned to his seat, placed my legs on his and leaned back against the log he had been leaning against, holding me in place.

"What are you doing? Let go of me!" I whispered so as not to wake the others.

"You're more comfortable with your feet up, right? It'll do your leg good."

Without further ado, he covered his face with the brim of his hat and closed his eyes. I could get up and go somewhere else to show this meddling cowboy that I didn't like being picked up and carried around like a doll, but the truth was that I was quite comfortable, so I decided to imitate him. I leaned my head against the rock, covered my face with my hat, and closed my eyes. I was beginning to feel drowsy when the weight of a hand on my thigh, its warmth coming through the fabric of my jeans, made me open my eyes with a start.

"What are you doing?" I repeated breathlessly, lowering my voice even more.

"I'm massaging your leg. Your muscles are stiff."

I shook my leg to push him away, but he wouldn't let me. "Seriously, let go of me!"

But he held on. "Just relax, princess. You'll thank me later."

The truth was that the gentle massage was rather agreeable.

"You take too many liberties, cowboy." Despite my disapproving tone, the sensation was so pleasant that I stopped resisting. I leaned back against the rock and let out a sigh of pleasure. "I don't know what you're up to, but I know you're up to something."

I peered under the brim of my hat and caught the flash of white teeth as he smiled.

"It's simple. I intend to woo you."

"Woo me?" I sat up quickly and pulled my hat back to see if he was laughing at me. Then I looked around to see if anyone had heard us, but fortunately everyone was at a safe distance.

"You'd think you'd never heard the word before," he said good-naturedly.

"For your information, 'woo' is a rather old-fashioned word."

"Not for me." And he added abruptly, "What about Eric, didn't he ever woo you?"

This time I wasn't going to play his game of trying to get information from me about my ex at the slightest opportunity, so I answered calmly, "To be honest, I don't remember. We had been together too long. But judging by the stories my friends in Los Angeles tell, wooing is pretty much out of fashion these days. According to them, men look at you funny if you don't have sex on the first date."

"You and I didn't have sex on the first date."

"Maybe it's because 'you and I' have never been on a date ?" I replied with a smirk.

He smiled again. "Maybe that's the reason."

"And why do you want to woo me?" I wasn't going to let him get away with that.

"Why would I? For the obvious, of course."

I suppressed the urge to make a snarky comment; it wasn't lost on me that he was trying to get on my nerves.

"Take me to bed?" I tried to sound as nonchalant as possible. "You know I'm willing to sleep with you, you don't have to go to all this trouble."

This time I managed to get a reaction. Vance sat up straight against the tree trunk, took off his hat and ran his fingers through his thick dark hair before putting it back on.

"But I don't just want to sleep with you." His words, spoken in the same indifferent tone as if he were talking about the weather, made me frown.

"I know you're pulling my leg, but if you're even remotely serious, I've already told you that love is over for me. Too much suffering. I don't plan to fall in love ever again."

"You don't?" He scratched his jaw thoughtfully. "Maybe it's not up to you."

"Of course it's up to me!"

"We'll see." Without further ado, he stood up, shook out his pants, and yelled, "Let's go, guys!"

And I was glad – or maybe not – to finally put an end to this ridiculous discussion that was going nowhere.

I don't think I'll ever forget the sight of that huge black and brown tide crossing the river ford amidst the mooing of the animals and the whistling encouragement of the cowboys. Thanks to the expertise of the Double B men, this seemingly impossible task was accomplished in what seemed to me to be record time.

"It's amazing, don't you think?" Carol's face broke into a huge grin, but I was so overwhelmed by the incredible scene unfolding before my eyes that I just nodded my head. I felt like one of those daring pioneers of yesteryear.

"Come on, now," Carol said after a while, digging her heels into her horse. She must have noticed my uneasiness, because she added, "Don't worry, I'll go first. If Maya sees that you are confident, she will follow my Bella without hesitation."

I nodded again and concentrated on following her instructions. A few minutes later, I had crossed the river with no more mishaps than a few splashes of icy water on my pants.

"Very good, princess."

I lifted my head to find Vance watching us from Ranger's saddle. When I realized that he had been prepared to intervene in case of emergency, I was overcome with a strange warmth that I tried to hide behind a cocky attitude. "Did ya doubt it, cowboy?"

He gave me one of those dazzling smiles that melted my brain. "Never, princess."

Then he yanked on the reins to turn his mount and set off to cover one of the flanks of the herd.

"I've never seen Vance so intent on a woman."

Hearing Carol's comment, I reluctantly forced myself to look away from the galloping rider. "It's normal. I'm his friend's sister. I wonder how he was going to tell Raff that I drowned in the river.

"Yes, of course, that must be it."

I pretended not to notice her mocking tone and set off again.

13

The bulk of the mountains became more impressive as we approached them. The terrain became quite steep and we were enveloped by the pungent smell of conifers. As we climbed up into the mountain pastures, the air became colder. Zoe had told me that the average daytime temperature in this area of Wyoming was seventy-seven Fahrenheit in the summer, but that it could drop to thirty at night. In fact, the mountains were full of snowfields; shady areas where the snow didn't melt until well into the summer.

I managed to get my sweater on without having to restrain Maya, and told myself that I would need the shearling coat as soon as it got dark. Judging by the length of the shadows, it wouldn't be long before the sun went down completely. I was glad. The truth was that my whole body ached, especially my bad leg.

"We'll stop soon." Carol said as if she had read my mind.

Indeed, a few minutes later we stopped in the shelter of a vast pine grove. Carol dismounted nimbly, but I was so numb I didn't dare. I was still wondering how I was going to get off Maya without hitting my head on the ground when a pair of hands wrapped around my waist and lifted me out of the saddle as if I didn't weigh an ounce.

"How are you holding up?" Vance asked without letting go. I clung to his waist, afraid my legs wouldn't hold me, and grimaced.

"I don't think I'll ever walk again."

I heard his soft chuckle. "I'll help you take a few steps until the blood starts circulating again."

He wrapped an arm around my waist and I did the same. Together we made our way to the campfire that one of the men had lit, where Carol had already set up a huge cast-iron pot, and I collapsed in pieces on the grass.

"Maya..."

"Don't worry, I'll take care of your horse."

"Thank you," I said in a weak voice, I had no strength left to argue.

I did some stretches and rubbed my leg hard until the cramps went away a little. "Tell me what to do, Carol."

"Cut strips of bacon to add to the beans. Don't be shy about the size, make them plump. We're all starving."

As soon as they finished tending the horses and setting up camp, the cowboys eagerly approached the campfire, attracted by the delicious smell coming from the pot.

"Ready!"

Carol began filling the plates I had been assigned to serve, along with the appropriate spoon and a cup full of a concoction they called coffee that was so strong I couldn't help but grimace when I took my first sip. When they were all served, I sat down on a small rock and began to devour my ration. Those beans, so hot that I burned my tongue a couple of times, knocked the morning sandwich off my list of the most exquisite delicacies I had ever tasted, and once I got used to the bitter tang, I found the coffee delicious as well. I wasn't used to caffeine at night, but after such an exhausting day, I was more than confident that it wouldn't affect the quality of my sleep at all.

Conversation flowed around the campfire, often accompanied by loud laughter. The cowboys were like big kids and enjoyed playing practical jokes on each other. When we finished eating, someone took out a harmonica and the air was filled with the melancholy notes of old love songs. Once again I was reminded of those brave pioneers who pushed westward, crossing lands full of dangers in pursuit of vague dreams of a better life.

I helped Carol pack and we went to wash the pot and dishes. The temperature had dropped sharply, and once I was away from the comforting proximity of the flames, I had to pull the collar of my coat up to my ears. The camp was not far from the river, but the few yards that separated us from it felt very long. The sounds of the night, so unfamiliar to me, seemed disturbing, and I stayed as close to Carol as I could. After washing everything, we sat down on a rock. The moon had risen and the sky, without a cloud in sight, was dotted with thousands of tiny stars. I gazed at them in fascination; I was not used to the lack of light pollution characteristic of big cities.

"It's so beautiful," I barely whispered, as if afraid my voice would disturb such beauty.

"It is."

It was not Carol's voice that answered me, but a much deeper, more masculine one. Immediately I felt the weight of hands on my shoulders and I turned with a start.

"It's not funny, Vance. You scared the hell out of me." The truth was that my heart was pounding like crazy, although to be honest I wasn't quite sure if it was from the fright or the warmth of his hands.

Carol jumped to her feet. "I have to get back or Zoe will take up all the space in the tent."

"I also…" I tried to follow her, but Vance's hands, loose but firm, stopped me.

"Good night, Carol. I'll get the pots later."

"No need, big brother, I can handle it. Good night, sweet dreams, guys."

I don't know if it was my imagination, but I thought I detected a hint of mockery in Carol's words and I felt all the blood rush to my face. Fortunately, Vance was still behind me and it was too dark to notice.

"I'd better go to sleep too. I'm exhausted." I suddenly had a crazy urge to run.

"Not so fast, princess. Come, I want to show you something."

He grabbed me under my armpits and pulled me to my feet. Immediately I was facing him with my hands on my hips. "Do you always have to be so bossy?"

"Me? Bossy? I'm sure you've mistaken me for someone else."

Ignoring my obvious reluctance, he wrapped an arm around my waist and made me walk upstream. Over the crunch of twigs crushed by our boots, we could hear the hoots of night birds, the chirping of crickets, and the occasional moo.

"Let me go, Vance. My leg hurts and I don't want to walk anymore." I especially didn't want to be alone with him. I had a strange feeling in the pit of my stomach. It could have been the beans making me sick, but I was afraid it was something else.

"Sorry, I forgot about your poor leg for a moment." He bent down and hoisted me over his shoulder like a sack of flour.

"Vance!"

"It will only take a moment, princess. I don't know to which of my ancestors I owe this caveman streak," he said, walking at a good pace despite my weight and without ever getting out of breath, "but I do know that as soon as I see you, it makes itself felt."

Ignoring my protests, he carried me a long way, finally stopping and saying, "Close your eyes."

Dizzy from the uncomfortable position, I obeyed. Immediately he lowered me to the floor and turned me around.

"You can open them now."

I obeyed once more and looked around in bewilderment, unable to utter a single word. We were standing on a colossal, almost flat rock that jutted out like a balcony over the river. Beyond the mountains that loomed protectively above us, a dazzling full moon peered down, drawing silvery glints from the snow that sprinkled the peaks and the water of the river that flowed with deceptive stillness at our feet. If I had thought before that the stars were counted in thousands, from this natural observatory I would have spoken of millions. Millions of tiny dots that gave the celestial vault a milky appearance.

Breathless, I leaned against Vance's chest, who was still behind me.

"It's... I can't describe it," I said in wonder, turning to him with a smile. "Thank you for this incredible gift."

"It's not a gift."

Vance hadn't taken his hands off my shoulders and we were so close I could see the intense glow in his eyes.

"Ah, isn't it?" I tried to block out his disturbing proximity by concentrating on our conversation.

"Actually, I expect you to give me something in return."

I inhaled deeply in a vain attempt to remain calm and tried to use my most nonchalant tone, "Something like what?"

"Something like this." He cupped my face in his big hands and kissed me.

My first thought was, "How does he ever manage to keep the hat out of the way?" My second was, "Oh, my God!," and a moment later I could think of nothing else.

I understood how much I had wanted him to kiss me again when I found myself on my tiptoes, pressed tightly against his body, my arms around his neck, my fingers tangled in his hair, doing my best to pull him even closer. My passionate response seemed to unleash something that had been safely tucked away behind that impenetrable calm. Suddenly, the strong hands had ceased to be gentle and had become eager explorers, greedily taking possession of the new territory. With skill and urgency, he unbuttoned my coat and slid his hand under my shirt. The warmth of it gave me goosebumps. My nipples were so hard they ached and the calloused touch of his fingers on one of them made me arch desperately against him. A second later, he pulled his lips away from mine and, while still caressing one breast, began to suck on the other over my sweater. The sensation was so incredible that an uncontrollable moan of pleasure escaped my throat and mingled with the howl of a lone wolf.

"Aisha..." he panted hoarsely against my chest.

My hands had decided to explore under his shirt as well and at this moment they were eagerly caressing the hard muscles of his back. But that wasn't enough for me, I needed to be much closer to him to calm the burning inside of me.

"Vance..." I said his name in a pleading whisper, and that was enough.

The cowboy released me, but before I had time to protest, he took off his own jacket and spread it on the icy rock. Then he helped me to lie down on it and hurried to lie on top of me. With a sharp movement, he pulled my shirt and sweater up to my throat. Then, with impatient fingers, he pushed my bra aside, exposing my breasts, their whiteness visible in the darkness.

"God, you are so beautiful," he moaned in a raspy voice so close to my skin that the heat of his breath caressed my nipples and I felt them harden even more.

He placed his mouth on one of them again, and in less than a second, the chill that had come over me when I felt the cold air on my naked flesh vanished. Breathless, I tangled my fingers in the dark hair and opened my eyes. As I gazed at the splendor of the sky above our heads, I was seized by an almost primal thrill of belonging; belonging to this timeless place; belonging to the man who was devouring me with hungry caresses.

The cowboy's nimble fingers fumbled with my belt buckle and it wasn't long before he had my jeans unbuttoned. Impatiently, I lifted my hips to help him remove them. I couldn't wait another minute. Vance tugged frantically at the waistband of my pants, cursed angrily, and... stopped.

"Vance?" I wiggled my hips a little to urge him on, but he let himself fall on top of me, taking care to rest on his forearms so as not to crush me with his weight.

"We can't, Aisha."

"What do you mean we can't?" I couldn't even understand what he was trying to say. I was so blinded by desire that I couldn't think of anything else.

"If we make love, you won't be able to stay in the saddle tomorrow."

I couldn't believe it! That cowboy who promised but never delivered was rejecting me again. Was this another one of his twisted jokes? But Vance was deadly serious, and I noticed he was breathing hard.

"And may I ask why you didn't think of this before?" My voice sounded a little too loud in the silence of the night.

"Aisha, it's hard for me to think when you're around."

"Don't give me that, smartass." I was so angry my voice was shaking. "You did it on purpose. To turn me on, to show your power over women. Over every woman."

"I assure you, my ten percent of burning Mexican blood is about to reach boiling point. You really think I'd play with this?" He rubbed his hips against mine, and as angry as I was, I had no trouble feeling how turned on he was. "And if you're thinking of revenge, forget it. My chivalry has its own penance. A painful penance," he stressed in a husky voice.

"Chivalry? Ha. To play with a woman's emotions in this way is most base."

“I can see you’re a spoiled brat, incapable of empathizing with those who truly suffer.”

Then the traitor lowered his head and kissed me, and though I was furious, I kissed him back while caressing his buttocks over his pants, unable to contain the passion he had unleashed in me.

Much later, Vance pulled away again, and when I heard the brutal curse that escaped through his clenched teeth, I couldn’t help but smile. At least I’d managed to get that smartass off his rocker.

“Aisha Brooks, you are... a bad woman,” he said with a strangled sigh. “You’ve tempted me beyond a man’s endurance. Tonight I have no choice but to let you go, but you know the saying: revenge is a dish best served cold.”

I let out a mischievous chuckle.

With a sigh, he put my bra back in place and leaned in once more to plant a final kiss on each of my breasts. With another deeper sigh, he pulled down my shirt and sweater and helped me to sit up. To avoid further temptation, I quickly fastened my pants and belt and buttoned my coat up to my chin. It took a little longer than I thought. My fingers were trembling, and it wasn’t just the cold.

“You know what struck me most about our… exchange?” I said with feigned nonchalance as we walked back to camp holding hands.

“My sex appeal? My mastery as a lover?”

"Cold, cold." I shook my head. "What surprised me most was that your hat never moved from its place."

"Well, how disappointing."

I knew he was smiling, and I smiled too as he lifted my hand to his mouth and kissed my palm passionately.

The next morning it was a real struggle to open my eyelids. The three of us girls shared a tent, and Carol had to call us several times before she managed to wake the rest of us. Judging by the goofy grin that wouldn't budge, it was clear that Zoe was enjoying her romantic moment in the wilderness as well.

It was hard to leave the warmth of the sleeping bag, and I didn't stop groaning for a second as I pulled on my boots, much to the amusement of my companions who had camped many times before and were used to the discomfort. Then, each with a bar of soap and a towel in hand, we laughingly made our way to the area of the river most sheltered from prying eyes, where we washed as best we could. I did not stop chattering my teeth for the duration of my morning toilet.

Carol finished quickly because she still had to prepare the coffee and cookies for breakfast, and Zoe was in a hurry to see Brad again, but I, who, to be honest, wasn't going to be much help other than handing out the cups of coffee and cookies when everything was ready, decided to stay a little longer.

The ethereal shreds of mist floating on the water and between the tree branches gave the landscape an enchanted air. I half expected to see a pair of wood elves emerge from under a rock. Humming a song, I walked upstream for a few minutes, trying to locate the rock where Vance had made me lose my head the night before, making out its jutting shape in the distance.

I would have liked to go there and relive the passionate scene, but I decided against it. Surely the coffee was ready by now. I was silently saying goodbye to this magical place when the icy brush of metal next to my ear paralyzed me.

"Well, well, well what have we here?" I recognized the mocking voice immediately and my heart skipped a few beats.

Very slowly, the barrel of the rifle almost glued to my temple, I turned to Colin and could not suppress a gesture of horror as I looked at his battered face. The swelling was almost gone, but he still had a black eye and a completely deviated nasal septum. Colin Hilton would never again be the cowboy with the perfect features that drove the girls crazy.

"You don't like what your little friend did to me, do you?" The almost black eyes blazed with hate, but he immediately pulled his mouth back into a wicked grimace. "He won't like what I have in mind for you either."

"I..." I was scared to death, but I made an effort to control the trembling in my voice and tried to reason with him. "You already made me pay with that drug you put in my beer. You'd better leave it alone if you don't want to get into a real mess, I..."

He pressed the barrel of the gun hard against my head and I shut up right then and there.

"That's the way I like it. You're prettier with your mouth shut."

"Put the gun down."

When I heard Vance's voice, I almost screamed with joy. I had been so focused on the tense exchange that I hadn't seen him coming, but it was too soon to declare victory.

"No, you put the gun down if you don't want me to blow your girl's head off." I had completely forgotten about the bastard's inseparable sidekick, who was also aiming at my head a few yards away with his feet firmly planted on the ground. He must have been hiding the whole time.

Vance considered the situation for what seemed like the longest seconds of my life.

"I'll drop the gun, don't hurt her." Very slowly, he bent down and carefully placed the rifle on the ground."

As soon as he straightened up, Colin pulled his elbow back without warning and slammed the butt of the rifle into his stomach. Vance doubled over with a strangled groan. I opened my mouth to scream, but Colin's buddy covered it with a not-so-clean hand and stopped me.

"Not here," he warned his friend, who at that moment was fingering the trigger of his gun with an expression that terrified me.

Colin muttered an oath. "You're right." And looking menacingly at Vance, he said, "You'll get yours later."

He approached me with a sinister smile, and the other one let me go, still aiming at Vance, who was still clutching his stomach and breathing heavily.

Colin gagged me with my own bandana and tied my wrists with a piece of rope he had taken from his jacket pocket. Then he did the same to Vance, though he tied his hands behind his back.

"Let's go." He accompanied the command with a strong push that almost knocked him down.

We walked through the pines to where they had hidden the horses. There were only three, already saddled, and when I realized that kidnapping Vance had not been in their plans, I was even more frightened.

Colin got on his horse and pointed his rifle at us. "Up you go. You'll have to share."

I didn't know how I was going to get on the horse with my hands tied, but Joker – I remembered his nickname as soon as I saw that wicked grin – solved my dilemma.

"Hold the mane."

I obeyed. With his help, I placed my left foot in the stirrup and he propelled me upward, subjecting me to a humiliating grope. I protested angrily, but the gag turned the insult into an unintelligible mumble that drew a laugh from him as he tightened the reins to the pommel of the saddle.

I soon forgot my humiliation, however. I was too distracted trying to figure out how Vance was going to get on the horse without help. I pulled forward as far as I could, trying to make as much room as possible, but I need not have worried. With incredible agility, he managed to get on behind me and stay on the horse, which had taken a few steps forward, frightened by the unexpected weight.

I could tell that Colin was anticipating at least a few humiliating falls, because he hit his mount with unnecessary force to get it to move forward. We followed behind him, with Joker bringing up the rear.

Although I was very worried about what that bastard might do to him in revenge, I was comforted by the feeling of Vance's solid presence behind me. In fact, it was he who was guiding the horse with no help other than his legs; I was just clinging desperately to the reins.

Colin led us up a rocky trail that got steeper and steeper. I imagined it would be easier to erase our footprints on this kind of terrain and I swallowed hard. We were moving very fast, and I realized with a lump in my throat that by the time the people in the camp realized that something had happened to us, we would already be well ahead of our rescuers.

The fog thickened as we climbed, drowning out the sounds of our mounts. It was so thick that at times I lost sight of the rider in front of me. I felt like we had been climbing for hours, and judging by how numb my hands were, the temperature must have dropped at least ten degrees. The trail got steeper, and at one point, as the fog lifted, the sight of the deep ravine less than two feet to my left made my mouth dry. I was also hungry. I hadn't even had a chance to drink a cup of hot coffee, but most of all I felt like crying.

As if sensing my mood, Vance rubbed his chin against my shoulder, and that affectionate gesture made me want to cry even more.

"How unfair it all is," I said to myself with a mixture of anger and despair.

After nearly three years of living in a state of mind that fluctuated between utter demoralization and the deepest rage, I had recently regained a taste for life. Once again, however, fate, karma, or whatever it was, was laughing in my face. From the looks and nasty comments of those two, I had little doubt of what they intended to do to me. If my chances of surviving the kidnapping didn't seem too flattering, I was aware that Vance's were practically non-existent. Even in the unlikely event that we both made it out alive, who knew what horrible permanent damage would be done to us after a never-ending series of torture and rape. Still trembling, I forced myself to put the dreadful thought out of my mind.

I had not made love to Vance – and the opportunity would probably never come again – but I had an almost superstitious conviction that the union of our bodies would have healed the wounds of the past. That after it happened, I would be free at last. Free to start a new life, free to love and be loved, free to be happy again.

At that moment, I promised myself that if by some miracle we made it out of this unscathed, I would not let any more time pass and I would take matters into my own hands, no matter what that stubborn cowboy said. I clenched the gag between my teeth and nodded resolutely.

The truth was that there was no point in worrying about the future, what was needed was to concentrate on the present and find a way to escape.

14

When we finally stopped near a set of rocks jutting out a few feets above the steep terrain, I was half unconscious. Fatigue, physical pain, stress, and cold clouded my mind. Colin dismounted, approached our horse and said something, but I stared at him blankly.

"Get off the horse. If I've to help you, I warn you I won't be very gentle." This time I understood, but the ground seemed far away and my limbs were so stiff that I could not move them.

"Mmm."

I realized that Vance had managed to dismount and that he was close enough to brush his chest against my left leg. I guessed from his head gestures that he wanted me to lean against him. Dazed, I wondered where he'd left the hat, but remembered almost immediately that it had fallen off when Colin hit him and hadn't let him pick it up. With great effort, I let go my numb fingers from the pommel of the saddle and wrapped my arms around his neck. The pain was terrible, but

I didn't allow myself to dwell on it and I dismounted without too much grace.

My legs gave out and I ended up hanging from Vance's neck. Literally. With my forehead pressed against his chest, I tried to move my legs to get the circulation going. Another series of painful cramps brought tears to my eyes, but after a few minutes I managed to hold myself up. Seeing that I was a little more secure, Vance bent his head to help me unhook my arms.

"Well done." Colin's buddy, looking more like the Joker than ever with that horrible grin of his, slapped the butt of the rifle with his palm as if clapping his hands.

"We'd better not light the fire tonight." Colin's words made my heart sink, but at least they had the virtue of wiping out Joker's nasty grin.

"No shit, dude, I'm chilled to the bone in this goddamn fog. Plus, we have a big head start on them."

"Maybe, maybe not." Colin shrugged. "I'd advise you not to underestimate Miguel. He's one of the best trackers I know. He was in I don't know what elite corps in the army." He began to unsaddle his horse and, without turning around, ordered dryly, "Tie them up somewhere where we can keep an eye on them and take care of their horse."

Joker didn't seem very happy with these orders, but he obeyed, cursing under his breath. He pointed to Vance and motioned for him to step in front with a nod of his head. Then he grabbed my arm and forced me forward toward some lonely dry pine trees a few yards from the rock shelter they had chosen for themselves and the horses. I prayed with all my might that he would tie Vance to me, and the fellow seemed to read my mind.

"You here and your studmuffin in there. I don't want you two doing dirty stuff tonight while I have to stand guard." More than the crude remark, it was the way he scanned me with those slightly crossed eyes that made me shiver violently.

Our captor wrapped the rope around Vance's shoulders and tied him to the trunk of one of the trees, and as if that wasn't enough, he tied his ankles as well. He'd left the rifle on the ground to keep his hands free, and I focused all my attention on it, trusting that he'd eventually be distracted and I'd be able to grab it. But Joker was quite meticulous, and even if I could have gotten my hands on the gun, I didn't know how much use I could put it to with my wrists tied.

But there was no need to fret, because Joker repeated the same operation on me. He squeezed the rope so hard that I could hardly breathe, but at least he didn't tie my legs. He took the opportunity to grope me as much as he could and although I tried to defend myself by kicking him, all I got was his arm holding my legs and he laughing at me again.

"Too bad Colin has to go first, I like little shrews. I'll be waiting impatiently for my turn."

Then he leaned over me and licked my cheek with his tongue while giving me a painful pinch on one breast.

I shuddered in disgust and helplessness, but luckily Colin called him at that moment and he left me be.

I clenched my jaw and blinked several times to hold back the tears. When I managed to regain control, I looked at my fellow captive. The wind had picked up. The full moon peeked through the increasingly threatening clouds and illuminated his face. His eyes were fixed on me with an expression that made me catch my breath. It was then that I understood what Carol had meant when she said he had the word 'murder' written all over his face.

We stayed like that for I don't know how long, and I felt like we were communicating without words. It was as if he was telling me to be calm, that he would do whatever it took to set me free, and even though I knew for a fact that there was nothing he could really do, the thought comforted me.

I must have dozed off because I didn't see Colin arrive until a painful kick to the sole of my boot made me open my eyes and look around in terror.

"I didn't give you permission to sleep, did I?"

Filled with apprehension, I watched as he crouched down beside me. He was holding something that looked edible, and I began to salivate. I was hungry and thirsty; it was already dark and I hadn't eaten or drunk anything since the day before.

"You're hungry, aren't you?" He held what looked like a piece of beef jerky in front of me with a mischievous grin.

I just glared at him. That idiot had another thing coming if he thought I was going to beg. Actually, it was more than likely that I would end up groveling at his feet in a few hours, but for now, those bastards had not completely broken my spirit.

He seemed to read the defiance in my eyes, for without the slightest gentleness, he released my gag and shoved the beef jerky into my mouth, hurting me. I figured he wouldn't take it too well if I spat it in his face, so I started chewing slowly.

When I managed to swallow the hard, salty piece, I asked in a hoarse voice, "Aren't you going to feed Vance?"

"My mother wouldn't like that, she always says not to waste food."

A sentence like that left little room for doubt, especially when it was accompanied by a crazy gleam in the dark eyes, but I pretended not to notice.

"Can I have some water?"

He pulled out the canteen he carried over his shoulder on a leather strap. He uncapped it and held it to my lips. I drank greedily, but he took it away too soon. Then he forced me to eat two more pieces of meat, but when I begged for more water, he said that was enough.

"I think you know what to expect by now." He didn't lower his voice, it was clear he wanted Vance to hear everything.

I bit my tongue to keep from replying impertinently, "I have little imagination, thank God. But it smells fishy." I didn't think Colin would appreciate my dark sense of humor, so I just shook my head.

He pulled out a pocket knife, snapped it open, and I froze at the sight of the intimidating gleam of steel so close to my face.

"You're lucky Miguel is such a good tracker. I don't have time to do everything I want to do to you right now, but as soon as we're in a safe place, I promise you pain, lots of pain." Very slowly he traced a map of lines on my forehead and cheeks with the tip of the sharp blade, and although I had been shivering for hours, the violent shudder that shook me from top to bottom had nothing to do with the night temperature. Noticing my reaction, he let out a sinister chuckle. "Then I'll leave what's left of you to Joker; fortunately he's not too picky."

You have it tough, I said to myself. A psychopath and a rapist, what an unattractive combination. But as much as I tried to make a joke out of it, I was terrified. So scared that I could only stammer out my next question.

"What are… are you going to… do with him?"

"I'm going to give him a taste of his own medicine until he dies of an overdose." He laughed, it was clear that he thought his joke was very funny.

"Don't you think it's a waste?" I made a superhuman effort to sound calm. "You could get a good ransom for him, after all, he is the owner of the Double B."

He gave me the smile of a proud father at the comment of a smart child.

"I thought about it, don't think I didn't. But more than the money, I'm seduced by the idea of getting him a front-row seat to what I'm going to do to you. He beats me up, and in return I disfigure the girl he likes until the mother who bore her doesn't recognize her. Pure poetic justice," he said in a dreamy tone as he gagged me again. "Unfortunately, he's too dangerous. I know his tricks and I know that it will be difficult to keep an eye on him all the time, especially considering that his men cannot be far away. But…" He yawned and stood up again. "It's been a hard day, so I'll leave you to think about how interesting the next few days are going to be. Now rest… if you can, of course."

With a last chuckle, he headed toward the rocky outcrop they had chosen as a shelter from the night's cold and from which they could easily watch us. We, on the other hand, had no protection other than the dry pine trunks to which we were tied, and although the bonds on my wrists were not too tight, my hands were numb again. In addition, the rope dug into my chest every time I breathed. I could not remember ever being so cold. I kept shivering and my teeth were chattering. Luckily I was wearing my coat, but I wasn't sure if I could endure the near-zero nighttime temperatures. To make matters worse, it started to rain.

At first it was just a few drops here and there, but soon it became a downpour. I heard thunder in the distance and realized that a storm was brewing. The curtain of water barely allowed me to see Vance, but I noticed that he was struggling furiously with his bonds. I had also struggled with them, but had to give up when I realized that my efforts were in vain and only served to exhaust me more. So I was stunned when I heard his voice above the sound of the rain and wind.

"Be calm, Aisha."

I wanted to ask him how he had managed to get rid of the gag, but all that came out of my throat were unintelligible sounds. An overwhelming feeling of hope came over me and I struggled again to free myself. The wind had picked up, thunder rumbled closer, and lightning broke through the darkness of the night. Terrified, I closed my eyes and tried not to think about how much we were at the mercy of the elements.

"It's me," the same voice repeated, this time so close to my ear that I wondered if I was dreaming, but just then I noticed a slight tugging at the bandana and realized it was his fingers struggling to untie the knot. They must have been as numb as mine, because it took him quite a while to untie it.

"Vance!" I almost cried with relief when I was free of the gag.

"There's no time to lose, Aisha. The storm is almost upon us."

Suddenly, the rope holding me to the trunk loosened its grip and fell slack around my waist. I was free! Vance grabbed my hand and pulled me to my feet. I staggered, still not quite believing it, and turned to face him. All I wanted at that moment was for him to hug me, but he only gave me a gentle push.

"Hurry! We are in serious danger."

"As if I hadn't noticed by now," I said to myself, annoyed.

However, the deafening crash of thunder at that very moment reminded me that now was not the time to argue. I tried to take a step, but if the cowboy hadn't caught me in time, I would have fallen on my face and probably broken my nose. My limbs were so stiff from the cold and immobility that I doubt I would have had the reflexes or the strength to stop the blow.

Vance bent down, as on another occasion of more pleasant memory, carried me over his shoulder and ran toward a thinner clump of small spruce trees about fifty yards from the rocky outcrop. As soon as we reached it, he dropped me to the ground and took a few steps away.

"Stay away from me!"

I didn't like this order at all, especially when all I wanted was for him to hold me to his chest like a little child and reassure me that everything was going to be all right. On the other hand, it was pretty clear to me that we should have used the storm to get much further away. From our position I could still see the silhouettes of the horses, and Colin and Joker must have been lying down not far away, wrapped tightly in their sleeping bags.

Vance must have guessed my intention to sit on the wet ground, because he immediately fired off a fresh volley of orders, “Don’t sit down! Get as far away from the trees as possible and make sure only the soles of your boots touch the ground.”

Although I didn’t understand anything, I tried to follow his instructions. The air was filled with an unpleasant smell of rotten eggs and I noticed that my hair was electrified. Suddenly I saw tongues of bluish flame dancing on top of the dry pine trunks we had been tied to a few minutes earlier and heard a low humming.

“Vance!” I pointed my finger in that direction. At that moment, I also made out the silhouette of one of our captors, who had risen to his feet and was staring at the chilling spectacle with his hands on his hips.

“It’s the fire of San Telmo, get down!”

Stunned, I obeyed immediately and not too soon. There was a deafening roar, and seconds later, a bolt of lightning tore through the sky directly above us. Clutching my legs, I saw one of its branches reach the ground between the dry trunks and the rocky shelter. The ground shook beneath my feet and the jolt knocked me to the ground. Almost at the same time, I heard a piercing scream of pain and the whinnying of a mortally wounded horse.

“Are you all right?” I heard Vance’s voice over the ringing in my ears.

Was I all right? I didn’t know. I moved my legs, my arms, my head… and I was deeply relieved to feel no pain.

"Aisha, answer me! Are you all right?!" His concern made me feel a little better, and the lashing of the rain on my face helped me clear my head.

"Yes, I'm fine!"

"Well, don't just lie there, get back in position!"

With a grunt I squatted down again. I was soaked and every bone in my body ached, but the truth was that the storm was still roaring with intensity, and although they say that lightning never strikes twice in the same place, the powerful electrical apparatus that accompanied the storm made me doubt the popular wisdom.

I don't know how much time passed. I tried to stay as crouched as possible, with my arms around my legs and my forehead resting on my knees. I must have succumbed to exhaustion at some point, because the touch of fingers closing around my arms startled me.

Vance pulled me to my feet, and this time he wrapped me in a suffocating embrace that felt like heaven. Clinging to his waist, I opened my eyes to see that the rain had stopped. The wind had also died down and only the distant rumble of thunder could be heard.

"It's over, we're safe," he whispered hoarsely into my ear.

"Safe?"

"Colin and his buddy are dead."

Surprised by the unexpected news, I looked up at him.

"Dead?" I echoed him again in disbelief.

"Apparently they didn't know much about dealing with a thunderstorm on a mountaintop. The idiots chose the worst possible shelter. Rocks attract lightning just as much as solitary trees, and animals, like humans, are great conductors of electricity."

"But the lightning struck right in front of us, I saw it."

"Lightning does not usually strike an object or person directly. More often it hits the ground; the electricity spreads over a wide area, and if it encounters a person or animal in its path, it can travel up one leg, through the body, out the other, and jump to the next living thing nearby. That's why I told you to stay away from me.

"Are you sure they are dead?" I still couldn't believe such a miracle. I never thought that I could rejoice over the death of a human being, but the truth was that I wanted to scream with joy.

"Dead as a doornail. I think it was a cardiac arrest. The horses are also dead."

This news saddened me much more, and suddenly I had a disturbing thought. "How will we manage without the horses? I don't think I can walk back."

"Don't worry about that now. I've brought some blankets and food. We'll find a good place to camp, come on."

He slid an arm around my waist and helped me walk. I don't think even during the long hours of training in my *prima ballerina* days I had ever felt my muscles so stiff. I had to bite my lips to keep from screaming in pain every time I leaned on my bad leg, but finally we came to a sheltered spot that the cowboy found suitable.

I fell to the ground. So wiped out that I couldn't even bat an eyelid, I watched him go back and forth looking for branches that weren't too wet. Within minutes a few logs were smoldering in front of me. With a sigh of relief, I reached out my icy hands for the warmth of the almost invisible flames, thinking that I had never heard a more comforting sound than the crackle of that campfire.

Vance had made two more trips to the rocky outcrop where our kidnappers' bodies lay, and a pot of coffee was gurgling on the fire. As soon as the coffee was ready, he offered me a metal mug filled to the brim and some hard oatmeal cookies. I eagerly devoured the cookies, helped by long sips of coffee, not caring that it burned my tongue. It was amazing what a little warmth and a full stomach could do for a person. As soon as I took the last sip, I felt revived.

I glanced over at Vance, who at that moment was leaning over the campfire to refill the cups, and found him quite different without his hat. The flames played with his masculine features, illuminating some areas and leaving others in shadow, and once again I detected in his firm contours that thirty percent Sioux blood of which he boasted so much. To tell the truth, I found him more attractive than ever.

We were so tired that we barely spoke as we ate, but the food and the warmth of the fire and the coffee took away much of the terrible weariness that didn't even let me think straight.

"How did you manage to untie yourself?" I broke the silence as I wrapped the blanket he had thrown over my shoulders tightly around me.

Vance raised his hand to his head, but unable to find his hat to pull it back with his usual gesture, he settled for running his fingers through his soaked dark hair.

"You see, my father was always afraid that someone would try to kidnap me. A few years ago, the meat market wasn't so good, and a lot of ranchers were forced to close down. Some of them were really struggling. In fact, when I was about ten years old, he received a series of anonymous threats demanding money in exchange for protection. So during the annual week we spent in the mountains, in addition to learning survival techniques, Miguel was busy teaching me other tricks. Like how to free myself if someone tied me up, or how to always have an ace in my boot.

He lifted the leg of his jeans, reached into the shaft of his boot and pulled out a small knife. The flames tore a flash from the sharp blade before he put it back in its place.

"Wow!" I said, not hiding my admiration. "And what's the trick to freeing yourself when someone ties you up? Seeing how things are around here, it might come in handy for me in the future."

The white teeth gleamed in a seductive smile.

"Relax, from now on I won't let you out of my sight for two seconds." Something about the way he said it made my skin tingle, but I made a face to hide it. "The trick," he continued, as if he hadn't noticed my nervousness, "is to breathe in hard and tense your muscles as much as possible while you're tied up. That way, when you let the air out and release the tension, the ligatures will not be so tight. Once I got my shoulders free, it was no problem to slip my arms under my legs, rip off my gag, grab my secret weapon, and cut the ropes at my ankles and wrists."

Told like that, it seemed so easy, but the number of bloody scratches and cuts that covered his wrists and hands had not escaped my notice.

"Your father had what is called 'foresight.'"

"Indeed he did."

I stared into the flames, still thinking how incredibly lucky we were. If it hadn't been for Vance showing up at just the right moment… if it hadn't been for his father's extraordinary foresight… if it hadn't been for that cowboy's skill and cool… Despite the heat of the flames, I shivered violently.

"Don't think about it, Aisha." The warmth of Vance's hand on my shoulder comforted me. As usual, he had read my mind. "Actually, there's something else you need to think about tonight."

I frowned uncomprehendingly. "About what?"

"About what's about to happen between you and me."

The burning expression in his eyes left no doubt as to the exact meaning of those words. Noticing the blood pooling in my cheeks, I swallowed before asking in a weak voice, "Now?"

"Now."

"But it's been a very stressful…" The truth was, I didn't even know what I was saying, the look in his eyes made me feel completely idiotic.

"I know. Maybe it's not what I would have chosen for our first…" He let the sentence hang in the air for a second, and a new rush of blood colored my skin. "Our first date?"

"Maybe we should save it for another time, we're both… we're both tired."

I bit my lip, why was I making excuses like that? When I thought I'd never get the chance to sleep with him, I could think of nothing else, and now that what I had waited so impatiently for was about to happen, I was doing my best to avoid it.

"Come."

Vance had not been idle while we talked. First he placed a couple of camping mats near the fire and then covered them with one of the blankets. He held out his hand, and like a puppet with no will of its own, I grabbed it and pulled myself up. He gently helped me lie down on the blanket and stared at me. Scared – well, maybe that wasn't the right word – of what was in his eyes, I propped myself up on my forearms and tried to put up some kind of resistance.

"We haven't showered…" I whispered. The corners of his eyes crinkled in that seductive way of his, and I felt myself melting. I tried again, trying to make myself heard over the deafening pounding of my own heart. "And we're not going to be very comfortable."

Vance pulled the other blankets closer, knelt in front of me, took off my hat, tossed it aside with a flick of his wrist, and began to unbutton my coat.

"You're right. It's been a stressful day, we're tired, we haven't showered and we're not going to be very comfortable." He took off my coat and turned his attention to my boots. "Besides, it's cold and we'll have to forget to undress completely."

He deftly pulled off my boots and took off his own and his jacket. Then he made me lie down again, laid his body on top of mine, taking care not to crush me, and spread the two remaining blankets over us without stopping to talk. I let him do as if I were in a trance.

"Yes, I agree with you. The conditions are not ideal." He took off my sweater and his fingers undid the buttons of my shirt one by one. I no longer felt cold; in fact, I began to feel an intense warmth in certain parts of my anatomy. "But it's difficult, if not impossible, to expect everything to be perfect."

He pulled up my bra and used the pad of his thumb to torture my nipple with a skill that elicited a moan from me.

"However, I also believe that there is no better time than the present." He lowered his head and caressed one of my breasts with his mouth and then the other. I felt as if I had died and was in heaven, but this heavenly bliss ended too soon. My tormentor raised his head and continued his monologue to which I barely paid attention, "Especially if one considers that we've already waited too long, don't you think?"

Desperately, I held his face in my hands and stared at him, even though I could barely make out his features in the darkness.

"Would you mind… shutting up, I can't… concentrate." The fact that my voice sounded completely out of breath seemed to belie my statement. "I don't like so much chatter at a time like this."

"Oh shoot, that 'don't like' wasn't on my list."

"Will you shut up for once?" I lifted my head and kissed him passionately, tasting the inside of his mouth with a hunger that went beyond desire.

"Oh yes, not another word." Feeling his husky laugh against my throat as I finally released his lips was the tipping point. My skin tingled and I felt a dull throbbing between my legs. I arched against him, grinding my hips against his to relieve it, and when I felt his erection against my pelvis, I nearly let myself go then and there.

Vance pulled away slightly and I let out a grunt of protest. I couldn't remember ever being so aroused. Again, I noticed his soft chuckle seconds before he pulled my jeans and underwear down with a sharp tug. He immediately took off his own, put on a condom, and lay on top of me again.

"I hadn't imagined our first 'date' like this. Had you?"

But I wasn't going to let him start the small talk again. Impatiently, I shook my legs vigorously until I managed to get my pants and panties completely off.

"That's the way it is, cowboy, so you better do a good job."

"I'll do my best."

Then I wrapped my legs around his hips and pressed against him. The cowboy no longer laughed. With a moan, he tangled his fingers in my hair and kissed me with an eagerness that might have frightened me if it hadn't matched mine. Maybe.

It wasn't a slow roaming over every inch of each other's bodies. It was not a lingering caress until we had memorized the erotic map of each other's flesh. It was not a marathon of impossible positions. It wasn't even a 'hit it and quit it' between two strangers having sex for the first time.

Vance plunged into me with a powerful thrust, filling me completely. He pulled out for a moment before entering me again with hard and fast thrusts, while I accompanied him with the same frantic rhythm. I don't know if seconds passed or if it was hours. I don't know if seeing death so close somehow affected my emotions. All I know is that I was flying higher and higher, faster and faster, and suddenly the universe stopped for an instant before exploding into a thousand pieces.

I clung to him and buried my face in his neck as the aftershocks of the earthquake shook me again and again. When the tremors finally stopped, I became aware of my surroundings again, completely satiated and with a strange feeling of peace.

"Aysha…" he whispered, but I was too exhausted to answer or move.

He continued in a very low voice, still stroking my hair, "I must confess that there were several moments when I thought that you and I would never be able to be like this: in each other's arms after making love as if only the present moment existed." Vance's lips caressed my ear as his husky voice vibrated inside, and I shivered again. "Maybe you were right; maybe we should have waited to go back to the ranch to rest for a few hours after this ordeal. Maybe our first 'date' should have been in a warm bed with a comfortable mattress after a long shower. But I have to tell you: I don't regret it one bit."

I pressed a little closer to him. I had no regrets either, and I was certainly determined to see if this incredible ecstasy was only a product of the novelty and relief of having emerged unscathed from a desperate predicament, or if, on the contrary, it would replicate itself every time we made love again.

My silent response seemed to be enough for him, and his next words were a reflection of my thoughts. "I could not leave the possibility of making love with you in the hands of an uncertain fate any longer, and now that I have tasted what it is like... I am determined to repeat it again and again."

"It was... incredible." Words were not enough to describe what I had felt.

"Yes," he kissed my hair, "incredibly incredible. I have a proposal for you."

"Indecent?"

"I told you before, I would never make you an indecent proposal."

"Geez." I pouted in disappointment, and though he couldn't see it in the dark, he laughed that husky laugh of his that had the power to awaken the sex-hungry beast I didn't know lived inside of me.

"I know a very special place. If you're not too traumatized by what happened, I'd like to go camping for a few days. Just you and me."

"Camping?" The possibility of spending a few days alone with him was very tempting, but after that endless ride, after the terror I had experienced before and during the storm, after knowing that not far from us lay the bodies of two men, victims of the same uncontrolled elements...

Truth be told, the prospect of spending more days in these wild mountains did not appeal to me very much. "I don't know if I like the idea. I have to admit that after these recent experiences, I am a bit repulsed by wild, open spaces. Besides, we have no food or sleeping bags or horses or…"

Vance ended this enumeration, which threatened to become interminable, in an expeditious manner. That is, he kissed me on the mouth, and I immediately forgot what we were talking about.

"Miguel will show up any moment." It was obvious that his faith in Fernanda's husband's ability to follow our scent was unshakable. "Between what those two bastards were carrying and what he'll bring, we'll have more than enough."

"And you'll have enough…" I stopped in embarrassment, but Vance picked up on my concern right away.

"Ever since I heard you were coming to the Double B, I've been carrying a pack in my pocket." Maybe I should have been offended by this cocky cowboy's confidence, but I laughed instead. "Besides, if we run out, I can think of other creative ways to have fun without risk."

It was incredible. Between the exhaustion of so many emotions, the warmth of his body, and how good it felt to be cuddled in his arms, I had struggled for a while not to fall asleep. But those words and the way he said them were enough to wake me up instantly. Unable to contain my desire, I pressed against him even harder, and without a word, Vance reached for another condom, put it on, and we made love again with the same urgency as the first time.

When I finally stopped trembling with pleasure, still clinging to him, I whispered against his throat in an almost unintelligible voice of exhaustion, "I think we're going to need all that creativity, cowboy."

The sound of his soft laughter was the last thing I heard before I fell into a deep sleep.

15

A sudden movement woke me. I opened my eyelids, and with my brain confused by the last remnants of sleep, I watched without understanding the menacing silhouette of the rifle Vance was pointing in the direction of some bushes to our left. For a few moments I was so frightened that I forgot to breathe, but I immediately recognized the voice coming from there.

"I almost took you by surprise," Miguel said.

Vance stood and brandished his rifle. "As you can see, you didn't."

Then another rider emerged from the thicket; it was Josh. I frantically fumbled under the blanket for my jeans, but realized with relief that Vance must have put them on sometime during the night.

"Colin and Joker?" Miguel asked.

"Dead."

The man just nodded in satisfaction, as if this news was exactly what he had expected.

"Dead?" Josh, on the other hand, could not hide his excitement. "How did you do it? Are you okay, Aisha?"

I nodded with a reluctant smile. Josh looked ready to subject us to a thorough interrogation, but his brother raised his hand for silence.

"I'll answer all your questions in a moment, Josh, but for now, let us prepare breakfast."

A few minutes later, the fire was lit and the coffee pot was set on a simple iron grate. As I smelled the delicious aroma, my stomach rumbled and I realized I was ravenous again.

In no time at all, Miguel, who had obviously learned a trick or two from his wife, had a succulent breakfast of fried bacon and freshly baked oatmeal cookies ready. As we enjoyed our second cup of coffee, Vance recounted what had happened since Colin and Joker had surprised us at the river, patiently answering the myriad questions from Josh, who didn't hesitate to interrupt him at every turn.

I was glad that he was the one doing the talking, as I felt like all the horrors had happened to someone else. However, I couldn't help but shudder more than once as I relived certain parts of the story, still unable to fully believe in our immense good fortune. On one such occasion, Vance placed his hand on my thigh in a reassuring gesture. His brother and Miguel exchanged knowing glances, and I felt my color rise. I immediately pulled my leg away, drawing one of those almost imperceptible smiles from the cowboy.

"We better get going." Miguel stood up and shook out the bottoms of his pants. "We have to call the sheriff, and if we don't hurry, they won't get here before dark, and by then the scavengers will have had their feast."

The casualness with which he spoke made me shudder.

"We're not going to wait for Tom and his men," Vance said as he tucked the bag of coffee and the sack of oats into the saddlebags of one of the horses.

"No?" Josh looked at him in surprise.

"Aisha has just been through a traumatic experience, I want her to recover a bit before she faces an interrogation. We've decided to camp around here for a few days." I noticed my color rising again and to hide it I lowered my head and started folding the blankets we had used the night before. "You can let Tom know what happened, tell him we'll stop by his office on Tuesday to finish filling him in."

"Tuesday? But there are three days left, are you sure Aisha wouldn't rather go to the ranch to rest? Fernanda and Carol will take care of her like a couple of broody hens. Besides, Tom won't like it at all, it's a kidnapping case. There are two dead..."

"Anyone with two eyes can see that Vance had nothing to do with their deaths," said Fernanda's husband, who had been watching Vance silently for some time, and added bluntly, "Tom will have to be satisfied with our explanations for the time being."

"But..."

"I'll take your horse." Now it was Vance who cut off his brother's protests. In one fluid motion, he swung the saddlebags full of supplies over Josh's saddle and fastened the blankets.

"My horse?"

"Come on, son, stop repeating everything your brother says and help me with this."

Miguel threw a sleeping bag at him.

"Ouch!" Josh caught it on the fly.

"Thanks." His brother snatched it from him and tied it to the saddle as well, checking one last time to make sure everything was secure. "I think we have everything we need. Aisha, are you ready?"

Of course I was ready, I couldn't remember a trip I'd ever taken with less luggage. I bent down to get my hat, put it on and walked over to the horse.

"By the way, Josh, you don't mind if I borrow this, do you?" Before the other could speak, Vance grabbed his brother's hat and put it on. "I'm afraid mine is still down by the river somewhere."

"I found it and gave it to Carol to keep for you," Miguel said. "I thought you'd miss it."

"Crap, Vance!" Josh protested. "The hat and the horse are things you should never borrow from a man."

"But you're my dear little brother." Vance patted him on the shoulder, and his brother had no choice but to accept the double loss with a snort.

"Up you go, princess!"

The cowboy grabbed me by the waist, pulled me onto the horse, and sat down behind me in one swift motion.

"Miguel, Josh, I hope you'll be able to live without me for a few days."

Vance pulled on the reins to force the horse to turn and we rode away at a leisurely pace.

"Don't worry, I'll be happy to be the one giving the orders for a change!" Josh's shout brought a smile to my face.

We followed the same path that had led us there, but at one point Vance turned off onto a barely visible trail. It seemed as if history was repeating itself: him behind and me in front, on the same horse, but of course nothing was the same. Now we could talk and laugh freely. Often the cowboy would put his mouth to my ear and whisper words that sometimes made me laugh and sometimes made me shiver, usually accompanied by a shower of kisses along my neck or a gentle nibble on my nape.

We advanced very slowly, talking nonsense. Occasionally he would point out a bird of enormous size that soared above us on the currents of air, or one of the deep ravines that cut through the terrain, terrible scars in the earth where it was enough to peer a little to be seized by a paralyzing vertigo, and he would tell me fascinating legends of the Indians who had inhabited these wild lands long before the arrival of the white man.

Time flew by, and at last we stopped at the entrance of a narrow gorge through which a shallow stream ran.

"Now you must close your eyes."

"Have I told you that I don't like being ordered about?" I said as I settled more comfortably against his chest and closed my eyelids.

"Only a few hundred times, I think."

I noticed him gently tap the horse's flanks with his heels and we set off again. I could hear the splash of the animal's hooves and wondered what surprise awaited me. I fought with myself not to cheat, but just then, and once again showing that disturbing ability he had to read my mind, the cowboy's warm hand covered my eyes.

We rode like this for a few minutes, and when I opened my mouth to protest this endless blind march, he took his hand away from my eyes and whispered next to my ear, "You can open them now."

I blinked for a few seconds, blinded by the sunlight.

"Vance…!" I said his name softly, marveling at the scenery before me.

The narrow pass had led us into what seemed like another world. Behind us were the high rock walls that blocked the sun's rays. In front of us stretched a meadow not much bigger than a couple of football fields, almost entirely covered with thousands of pale blue flowers. The previous night's storm had completely swept away the clouds, and the sun's brightness plucked sapphire sparkles from the deep waters of a small mountain lake that looked like a jewel set with precious stones.

I opened my mouth but could not utter another word. The untamed beauty of the place, untouched by any trace of human presence, had taken my breath away.

"Are you still repulsed by wild, open spaces?"

And suddenly I understood what this psychology-loving cowboy was trying to do: bury the bad memories under a ton of new and much more pleasant ones.

I turned to him, kissed him on the stubbly chin that was all I could reach, and just said, "Thank you."

Vance's slow smile that made his green eyes sizzle had a strange effect on my stomach. I shook my head in resignation; this cowboy was pure sin and I wasn't virtuous enough to resist. Resolutely, I slipped an arm around his neck, forced his head down and kissed him with desire. He kissed me back just as fiercely until a sudden movement of our mount reminded us where we were.

"If I had known the beauty of this place would have this effect on you, I would have brought you here much sooner," he said huskily, stroking my cheekbones with his thumbs before leaning in for one last kiss.

After a while we pulled apart laughing and he helped me down.

"I'm going to set up camp under those trees. If you want, you can take the opportunity to wash up, I'll do it as soon as I'm done."

More than trees, it was a row of overgrown bushes on the edge of the lake, but the sun was beating down hard and the little shade would be welcome. I looked around for a more sheltered place to wash up and found a lone rock a few feet away that might serve as a screen. Vance tossed me a bar of soap and a blanket, which I grabbed deftly and hurried away. The idea of finally washing myself was most enticing.

After a brief struggle, I managed to get my boots off and made sure I was adequately protected by the rock before removing the rest of my clothes. I stepped into the water, careful not to slip on the slippery boulders that made up the wall of the lake, and stifled a groan. The water was freezing. When it reached my mid-thighs, I decided not to go much deeper. In addition to soaping myself, I took the opportunity to wash my hair, but I think it was the quickest bath of my life. Shivering, I hurried out and wrapped myself tightly in the blanket with trembling hands before washing my underwear and shirt and laying them out to dry on the rock.

"Are you done?"

I looked up startled, so absorbed had I been in these chores that I hadn't heard him approach, and when I saw him standing next to me, my mouth went dry. He must have taken the opportunity to bathe as well, for like me, he was covered only by a blanket wrapped around his narrow hips. My eyes lingered longer than necessary on the muscles visible under the skin, which was slightly lighter than that of his hands and face, and on the fine line of dark hair that disappeared under the edge of the improvised towel. I swallowed and cleared my throat, trying not to let it show how much he turned me on just by looking at him.

"Is the food ready?"

"Not yet."

The green eyes never left my bare shoulders, and something I saw in them made me speak at full speed even though I had no idea what I was saying, "The water's freezing, isn't it? Wow, I'm starving."

"Me too."

He sat down next to me, lifting me onto his lap and draping one arm around my shoulders while his other hand rested on my knee. The warmth he gave off came through the thick fabric of the blanket and made me forget that I had been freezing to death just a few seconds before. Slowly, he bent his head and began to nibble gently along my neck. Goose bumps automatically appeared on my skin and my nipples stood on end. Shivering, I placed my palms against his bare chest and felt that searing heat again.

"Vance..." His name escaped my lips in a moan. "There's too much light, I..."

Another soft bite hit a particularly sensitive spot under my earlobe and I forgot what I was trying to say. I wrapped my arms around his neck and pressed harder against him. Vance lifted his head for a second, caught my mouth and tongued his way in. Mine came out to meet his and I thought, as I had on other occasions, that the cowboy knew how to kiss.

He slid a finger into the edge of the blanket and I immediately felt it slip away. That suddenly pulled me out of this nirvana of desire and, showing amazing reflexes, I managed to hold the blanket to my chest just in time and pull away from him.

"What is it?" he asked, his voice hoarse with passion.

"Vance... it's daytime... I... I don't know if..." I stopped talking and pressed the rough woollen cloth to my chest, not knowing how to continue. I didn't like the idea that my attitude might make him think I was playing coy. But I should have known better by now; he caught on right away.

"Let's see..." With a tender look, he pushed aside a lock of soaked hair that had slipped across my face and tucked it behind my ear. "Thanks to the only 'date' we've had so far, I know you're not a prude..." I shook my head as I felt the blood rush to my face. No, that wasn't it. "And I don't think you're a vampire who hates sunlight either..."

Unable to hold his gaze, I bit my lower lip and shook my head again, but he held my chin between his forefinger and thumb, forcing me to look at him. "It's your leg, isn't it? You don't want me to see it."

It wasn't really a question, so instead of answering, I just swallowed.

"Do you think I'll stop wanting you if I see your scars?"

Of course I thought so, even I couldn't look at them when I showered.

"No one..." I cleared my throat nervously before continuing in a husky voice, "Apart from the doctors, only Eric has seen them, and you know how that turned out. Believe me, it's not a pretty sight."

"Aisha..." He framed my face with his hands and with his eyes fixed on mine, he said with impressive seriousness for once, "You are a beautiful woman; so much so that sometimes I cannot take my eyes off of you. Now that you have regained some weight, I can say without exaggeration that you have the sexiest body I have ever seen in my life."

If I had blushed before, now my face must have been a striking, garish red. The way he said it made it impossible to doubt his sincerity, and the way he looked at me made me swallow saliva again. It had been years since I had felt even halfway desirable.

"But..." He stopped.

I frowned. I didn't like that 'but' one bit.

"But?" I said in a whisper.

"But it's not just your looks that I like about you."

"Ah. No?" I tried not to look too interested, although I couldn't wait for him to continue.

"No. I like even more the passion you bring to life, how grumpy you can be, your courage, your stubbornness. You make me laugh and get on my nerves, all in the space of a minute."

"You have no nerves." I replied, unable to keep my mouth shut.

"You think so? Then why do I want to spank you and then kiss you until you're breathless every time we fight? Why did my hands shake the first time I held you? Why does my mind go blank every time I kiss you?"

"Really?" I could hardly believe it. I had always thought that Vance exercised iron self-control over his emotions.

"Really."

I leaned forward a little, resting my forehead against his and whispered, "I like that."

"I'm glad. Because I plan to keep kissing you, I plan to keep making love to you, and I plan to enjoy seeing your completely naked body."

I shivered in his arms and he noticed. "Are you afraid?"

"A little."

"You have nothing to be afraid of with me."

And I knew it was true. I had always felt safe with him.

"All right," I said very quietly, but he heard me.

"Then relax and let me do this."

I took a deep breath and let go, and for a woman who doesn't like to take orders, I think I did pretty well. Like a child, Vance grabbed me by the waist, lifted me into the air, and sat me down on the grass. Then he stood up.

"I'll go first."

I looked at him expectantly, I had no idea what the cowboy was up to.

"I'm going to show you all my imperfections, I don't want there to be any secrets between us. See this?" He pointed to a small scar, barely bigger than a scratch, on his side. "I got caught in barbed wire when I was four."

I rolled my eyes. This unnerving man was capable of taking me from deep emotion to the urge to burst out laughing in a matter of seconds.

"Hum. I can see you're not impressed, but you haven't seen everything yet..." He raised his eyebrows several times in a very expressive way before he hooked the edge of the blanket with his thumb and lowered it to the middle of his hip to show me the almost obliterated imprint of the stitches from an old operation.

"Acute appendicitis, eleven years old," he said proudly. "Impressed?"

"Very," I nodded in all seriousness, although what really impressed me was the sight of that muscular pelvis, which looked as if it had been carved out of marble.

Suddenly, with a gentle flick of his wrist, he dropped the towel and stood before me in all his glorious nudity and with unmistakable signs of being very, very aroused. My mouth went dry on the spot, but I could not look away.

"See, I have no more secrets from you." I shook my head, unable to say a word. Vance picked up the blanket that had fallen at his feet and spread it out on the grass. Then he bent down beside me, took me in his arms and gently laid me down on it. "Now it's your turn."

He slowly pushed me back until I was lying on the wet blanket. Then he took my hands and gently began to unclench my fingers, which I had inadvertently closed tightly over the blanket wrapped around me, one by one.

When I let go, he lay on top of me and ran the tip of his tongue along my collarbones. Very slowly, inch by inch, he slid the blanket down. First, he left my breasts uncovered and savored them thoroughly. Then, with a fine shower of kisses, he continued down my torso until he reached my navel. He lowered the blanket again and the warmth of his breath so close to those secret places made me clench my jaws to hold back a moan. Now only my legs were covered and in one swift motion he unrolled the blanket completely, pushing the ends aside.

I closed my eyes tightly and clenched my fists. I didn't want to see his revolted face when he saw my scars.

"Calm down, Aisha," he whispered after what seemed like an eternity, "I know your secret and I still think you are beautiful."

There was a world of tenderness in his voice, and as I felt his lips brush against my ugly scars, murmuring loving words, a tear slipped from the corner of my eye, and then another, and another, and another.

Suddenly it was as if I was participating in one of those ancestral rites of his shamanic ancestors. It was as if he was invoking the spirits of acceptance, forgiveness and oblivion through his gentle caresses... and an immense sense of peace washed over me.

"Open your eyes." I obeyed and met his less than an inch from my face. "You are a beautiful woman, Aisha, inside and out."

With a choked sob, I hugged him and kissed him with all my might. Vance responded with the same passion and a few seconds later he was inside me. Together we rose above the meadow, above these mountains, above the universe… and then we came down slowly, sweaty and exhausted, rocking gently in the last throes of pleasure.

"Thank you," was all I could say, my face buried in his throat.

Vance pulled me closer to him. "I'm the one who has to thank you."

It was then that I remembered something, "The food!"

We sprang to our feet, barely wrapped in our blankets, running barefoot and laughing our heads off to the makeshift camp, where the iron pot Vance had set on the fire gave off a suspicious smell of burning. We were so hungry, however, that we ate the stew, and despite the more than slightly burnt taste, did not leave a crumb.

16

For those few days I felt like an Eve who had returned to Eden. In fact, we spent more time naked than clothed. I had never been so isolated from the world as I was in that flowery meadow that Vance and Miguel had discovered on one of their mountain camping trips years ago, and not even when we drove the cattle to the mountain pastures had I lived in such primitive conditions.

All that time we never saw another soul. We were the only human beings for miles around and there was not a trace of modern civilization; not an antenna, not a signpost, not a hut... nothing. Man had not left his mark on this enchanted place.

The daytime temperature was very pleasant. We used to wake up late and start the morning with baths and games in the icy lake. Vance taught me to set traps. The first time I saw a rabbit caught in one, I struggled between pity and the urge to let out a cry of triumph. I insisted that the cowboy show me how to skin it, and though it disgusted me at first, I soon got the hang of it. That day we ate a delicious rabbit stew that I had made by myself. I had become a prehistoric woman, and the thrill of being able to survive in the wild in almost as primitive conditions as our ancestors did thousands of years ago made me feel powerful.

I could not remember ever laughing so much in my life; nor could I remember ever having such lively conversations with another person. At night, as soon as we finished dinner, we would curl up in each other's arms and with our eyes fixed on the dance of the flames, we would talk about everything under the sun, as if the small circle of light cast by the fire, in contrast to the darkness around us, created a bubble that isolated us from the world and unleashed our tongues.

Much later, under the blankets, we would make love until dawn, the cold completely forgotten, and finally fall into a deep and exhausted sleep.

But as always in life, everything, good and bad, comes to an end. We broke camp on the fourth day. When everything was packed, I looked around for the last time, trying to commit to memory every last detail of this beautiful place where I had been so happy.

"I'm so sorry to be leaving," I said regretfully.

Vance grabbed my waist and helped me onto the horse. "Don't worry, I promise we'll come back every year at this time."

I frowned slightly but didn't say anything, not wanting to spoil the good mood between us. In all this time, we hadn't made any plans. There had been no promises or in-depth discussions about the future of our relationship. As I saw it, the last few days had been a complete healing. The pile of negative emotions that had been building up inside me since I woke up in the hospital after the accident had disappeared without a trace. I hadn't felt this free in years. I no longer looked to the future with worry or fear, no longer looked to the past with longing and bitterness. Vance's caresses had brought me back to the present, to the here and now, and I felt that an existence full of possibilities was once again opening up before me.

From the way he looked at me, I think he sensed my discomfort, but he didn't say anything. He put one foot in the stirrup and climbed on behind me. We made our way back and I soon forgot about that almost negligible moment of tension.

The temperature was still very pleasant and the sun was shining high in the bright blue sky. We rode at a leisurely pace. I leaned against his chest, chatting and kissing at every turn. When we stopped for lunch, we made love again and laughed when we realized there was only one condom left in the box.

We arrived at the Double B as the sun was setting. Someone must have seen us and raised the alarm, because there was a whole welcoming committee waiting for us at the entrance to the ranch.

Vance jumped off the horse and helped me down, and within seconds I was sandwiched between Zoe and Carol, who were hugging me, laughing and crying at the same time. I suddenly realized I was crying too and was surprised at how close I felt to them, despite the short time we had known each other. I was so happy to be back, safe and sound, that I also hugged and kissed Fernanda with an affection that surprised me. When we parted, I saw her put a finger to her eyes to wipe away a furtive tear, and I smiled. Of course, the most reserved reception came from Vance's stepmother, who gave me a frosty kiss on the cheek, which I returned just as frostily. It was obvious that Tessa and I would never get along.

Vance, who had also been the subject of many warm, tearful hugs, held out the horse's reins to Josh and brought the emotional reception to a close.

"Shall we eat now? We're starving."

Of course, once we sat down to eat, the whole story had to be retold and countless questions answered, but the more we talked about what had happened, the more distant it all seemed. It was hard to believe that I had been one of the main characters in these dramatic events. The evening was one of the most lively I had spent at the ranch. I kept talking and laughing, and I couldn't help but notice Tessa's bewilderment at seeing me so animated, and the calculating look in her eyes as she turned them alternately to Vance and me.

It was late when we went to bed. The riding and the excitement had worn me out, and I thought I would fall asleep right away, but I was wrong. An hour later, I was still in bed with my eyes wide open, missing the warmth of Vance's body. Tired of tossing and turning, I pushed the covers aside, just as I heard a tapping on the glass of the door leading to the balcony.

I jumped out of bed and ran to open the door.

"You read my mind," I said to Vance, who stood on the other side of the door wearing only blue pajama pants.

The sound of his soft laughter was enough to send a rush of desire through me. I stood on my tiptoes, wrapped my arms around his neck and kissed him eagerly. He responded as if it had been centuries since we had kissed, and in one swift movement, he scooped me up in his arms and carried me to the bed.

Much later, with my head resting in the crook of his arm, I said in a sleepy voice, "You know, cowboy, I think I'm going to have a hard time falling asleep without you by my side."

He brushed my hair with the tip of his nose. "I don't think that will be a problem. I plan to sleep with you forever."

Suddenly I felt cold.

"I told you… I told you that I'm going back to Los Angeles as soon as the show is over. We both know this isn't real." I regretted those words as soon as they left my lips. The arm my head was resting on stiffened as his body tensed.

"What do you mean, 'this isn't real'?" He sounded as calm as usual, but I still got the impression that he was angry.

"I mean… What I mean…" I was confused. I didn't really know what I wanted to say. "Anyway, my stay here is just a pause. I've spent more time in the Double B than the judge ordered, so I think it's time for me to get my life back on track and decide what I'm going to do from here on out."

"So it's just been a 'pause' between us." I had never heard such a cold tone from him before.

I sat up a little, cursing the dim light coming through the French window that prevented me from reading his expression.

"Vance," I placed the palm of my hand on his cheek, "you can't imagine how much the months I've spent in the Double B have meant to me, and especially these days we've spent together. When I tell you that they have given me back my will to live, I am not exaggerating one bit. Thanks to you, I'm now able to accept my disability."

"You are not disabled," he interrupted me sharply.

"Well, in other words, to accept myself as I am now, to accept that I will never be a ballerina in any ballet. To accept my body, not to be ashamed of it, and even to be able to thank God for being alive, something that in recent years had felt more like a curse."

"Then why do you want to leave?"

"Because this is not my life, Vance!" I raised my voice a little. I didn't like being questioned about my motives when I didn't know them very well myself.

"Why not? You can make it your own whenever you feel like it. What ties you to Los Angeles?"

It was a good question, but I didn't have an answer and went off on a tangent. "I have to look for a job."

"Here's a job for you, Aisha. I need someone to do the bookkeeping for the Double B, and if that's not enough for you, I have another full-time job you might be interested in."

"Another job?" I thought for a moment and shook my head. "Forget it, I'm not much of a cook."

"I'm not offering you a job in the kitchen."

I frowned, confused. "So?"

In one swift movement, Vance was over me, pinning me down with his weight. His face was so close that I could see the glint of his eyes in the darkness.

"I want you to marry me, Aisha." His tone was urgent and I was speechless at this unexpected proposal. "I want to have 'dates' with you every night and every other morning. I want us to take long rides around the ranch. I want to go to work every day knowing that when I walk into the office, you'll be there, fiddling with the numbers. I want to come back to our secret meadow every summer, leave Fernanda and Carol to watch our kids, and make love to you over the flowers until we can't even move."

God, that was too much! For a moment I imagined a dark, serious little dark-haired boy and a naughty little blonde girl riding their ponies on the ranch while their parents played Adam and Eve in paradise, and the scene seemed so real it took my breath away.

"But getting married!" I repeated in disbelief. I was still unable to accept such a proposal. "It was the last thing I had expected. Until a few minutes ago, I was convinced that this was just a fling for you."

"I must have bigger communication problems than I thought if you really think that. Ever since I met you, I have tried to make it very clear that I did not want to make any indecent proposals to you. That I wanted to take things slowly, that I was courting you."

"I thought you were joking."

"And what happened between us these days, did you think it was a joke, too? Was it just a 'pause' for you, like you said before?"

When I heard his accusatory tone, I flinched as if I had been stung. It hurt that Vance had thought, even for a second, that our story was an unimportant episode for me.

"Of course not, of course it was important! I'm no Messalina, you know. You're the second man I've gone to bed with, for God's sake. It's just that I hadn't thought… it hadn't occurred to me…"

"That I could be in love with you."

It wasn't a question and I didn't have to answer; although the truth was that the idea hadn't even crossed my mind. I had been too focused on the avalanche of feelings and emotions that had been unleashed in my chest to worry about his.

"Well, I am," he continued firmly after a while. "I fell in love with you the night I went to your dressing room with Raff to congratulate you."

The silence lasted a little longer this time. I was so stunned by this revelation that I could not say a word, and it was he who broke it again.

"Love at first sight. The kind that, when you read about it in a novel, you say: impossible. But it is. Possible, I mean. I haven't stopped thinking about you since then, even though I've had sporadic relationships. I imagine Raff suspects something. He's always kept me informed of your movements and didn't hesitate to turn to me when you needed a place to get your strength back."

"I… I don't know what to say."

"Just say yes."

And I can't deny that I was tempted. Vance was a very attractive man and an imaginative and generous lover. Not only that, but he was a great person: thoughtful, intelligent, funny, courageous… the list was endless. If I had to give him a 'but,' it would be that he perhaps enjoyed laughing at me a little too much; in that respect he was very much like my brother Raff. But even though he could sometimes get on my nerves, deep down I didn't think that was an unforgivable vice either.

But he had spoken of marriage, of children; in short, of a lifelong commitment. Was I ready for such a step? Only a few months ago, I was still crying over Eric's betrayal and my failed dancing career, cursing the gods for my suffering. Was I really healed? Was I ready for such a radical change? I, the quintessential city princess, would have to live in the Double B, with the nearest town several miles away. And most importantly, I wasn't sure how I felt about Vance. It was true that I wanted him, that his caresses drove me crazy, but what I felt next to him was so different from my stormy relationship with Eric that I couldn't help but have doubts.

Vance was a good friend. He made me feel comfortable and safe. In our conversations, I could say the first thing that came into my head without fear of triggering a hecatomb. We could talk about anything without ending up arguing loudly, but was that love?

Eric was very intense; being the great artist he was, he was prone to emotional ups and downs. When he was in high spirits, life with him was wonderful and he could convince me of anything crazy. At other times, he would drag me down into abysses of despondency and bitterness. Anything could trigger one of these dark moods: an *échappé* that wasn't perfect, the broken elastic on one of his favorite ballet shoes, professional jealousy of a colleague or even of me. When it happened, I had to tiptoe around him and pray that the crisis would pass as quickly as possible. Living with my ex-boyfriend was like riding a roller coaster at full speed. It could be exhilarating at times, but other times it was just exhausting.

I too had experienced love at first sight and look how that turned out. When I first saw Eric at one of the rehearsals, I was dazzled, and it didn't take more than a few words with him for me to fall madly in love. It is true that I was very young; that I had no experience; that Eric was a very handsome man and a fabulous dancer; that I was proud that he chose me when he had so many others to choose from. Maybe I was naive, but I had given him my heart unconditionally, and he had given it back to me a few years later, terribly bruised, just when I needed his love the most.

But that was all in the past. I had already forgotten, hadn't I? For God's sake, I wasn't even sure how I felt about Eric, if I felt anything at all!

"I have to… I have to think about it."

Vance turned away from me and I heard him let out a deep sigh.

"When are you leaving?" he finally said. Now our bodies weren't touching, and even though I had the covers pulled over me, I felt cold.

"I was going to look for flights after the show."

"And have you, by any chance, stopped to think about what would happen to us?"

The truth was that I had been so caught up in the wonderful present that I hadn't had time to think about the future. In a vague way, I had taken for granted that our relationship would end as soon as I returned to my world. That in time, the magical days we had spent together would become a distant and sweet memory, like summer loves. One of those sweet memories that, when recalled, make you sigh with a smile full of tenderness.

"I thought… I don't know, I thought maybe we would see each other from time to time. You would visit me some weekend in Los Angeles, and I would spend a few days of my vacation here…

"Until, little by little, distance gave way to oblivion. I see."

It didn't sound so good, but I couldn't deny that this was what I had imagined. Once again, silence became another presence in the bedroom. It was incredible that in a few minutes I had gone from feeling like the queen of the universe to a human wreck, and Vance hadn't even raised his voice.

"Okay, let's do one thing."

I sighed in relief to see that he was not only still talking to me, but that he had apparently come up with a solution. "What do you suggest?"

"I realize that too much has happened to you in too short a time. You are also in an unfamiliar environment and I understand that you may have doubts. This is a very important decision that will affect all areas of your life. I think it would be good for you to take some time to clear your head."

"Actually, it would be good for both of us, don't you think?" I interrupted him a little annoyed. I didn't like him making me feel like a stupid little girl who didn't know what she wanted, even if it was true.

"Aisha, it is no sin to stop and think calmly." Even though I couldn't see him in the dark, I knew he was smiling and I couldn't help but roll my eyes. "And believe me, I don't need to clear my head. I know exactly what I want. I've known it for years."

This overwhelming certainty suddenly took away my desire to argue. "How long?"

"How about early fall? In the meantime, you'll have time to get organized, look for a job and… and say all the necessary goodbyes."

He didn't say it, but we both knew he meant Eric.

"And I won't see you in all that time?" My voice trembled. Suddenly, the idea of not being able to see him, hug him, talk to him, or even engage in endless discussions like we used to seemed terrifying. And then I realized that once again, as much as I hated to admit it, the cowboy was right: I didn't know what I wanted.

He put his arm behind my head again, and I clung to his chest, seeking the comfort of his warmth. "No, we won't see each other, but we'll talk on the phone a lot."

"But what's wrong with seeing each other on the weekends?" I protested.

"Aisha, if I come to visit, you know what will happen, don't you? We'll have sex until our brains melt."

That cowboy sure knew how to turn me on with a few well-chosen words.

"I don't know what's wrong with that," I said all cuddly as I showered his chest with kisses.

"I want you to have a clear head, Aisha. Marriage is much more than a little sexual attraction. Aisha! Aisha, you're killing me..." he moaned and I smiled against his skin. There was nothing I enjoyed more than seeing a man with such self- control lose some of it.

"It's okay..." My lips traced a slow line of kisses from his chest to his navel, and I was rewarded with another choked moan. "We'll do as you say: we'll wait for the fall."

Suddenly an idea came to me that I didn't like at all, and I raised my head.

"But until I leave, we'll continue with our 'dates,' won't we?" I felt his chest tremble under my palms and gave him a light pinch. "Don't laugh. It's not funny."

"What isn't?" He grabbed my arms and in a second I was the one trapped under his body. "You think I'd miss the chance to leave my imprint on you?"

"Imprint? You mean that thing Zoe told me about geese? The one about how they bond with the first thing they see when they hatch?"

"I see you're on your way to becoming a real country princess."

"I'm not a goose," I said, and to prove it, I lifted my head a little and kissed him full on the lips.

Vance kissed me back immediately, and the embers of the passion we had just shared flared into uncontrollable flames.

"You can bet I'm going to make the most of every last minute we have left," he said huskily before taking one of my breasts in his mouth and eliciting a deep sigh of pleasure from me. "I'm going to make love to you until you can't imagine making love to anyone else but me."

And true to his promise, we made love until the first light of dawn reminded us that it would be good to rest for at least a couple of hours.

17

With trembling fingers, I applied the last layer of mascara evenly, cursing as the brush slipped and smudged one of my eyelids. I grabbed some toilet paper to clean up the mess, and when I was done, I stared at my reflection in the mirror.

"Well, Aisha Brooks," I said aloud, "you look as pretty as you can look."

I turned and looked over my shoulder to make sure my bra strap wasn't showing through the round neckline in the back. I was wearing a sleeveless black dress I had bought for the occasion – in fact, the first dress I had bought in years – and tight stockings that hid the scars on my leg. Even though both the mirror and the saleswoman had assured me that it looked great on me, I felt insecure and wondered for the millionth time if it wouldn't have been better to wear pants.

I had been in Los Angeles for two months, and it was only now that I had worked up the courage to face Eric and finally get my feelings out in the open. I had taken tickets to the ballet three times. The first time I gave them away, the second time I managed to resell them online, but tonight I was determined to go to the premiere of *Giselle*, with Eric as Albrecht and his girlfriend as the young, innocent peasant girl. A bitter laugh escaped me at the thought of Antea as an innocent young girl.

I came out of the bathroom and glanced at the clock on the wall in the kitchen, which opened onto the living room of the small apartment. It was more than an hour before the show started.

I went to the refrigerator, which, like the rest of the furniture, was tiny, and poured myself some iced tea. Maybe a drink would have been better to calm my nerves, but there wasn't a drop of alcohol in the whole house.

I had rented the studio in the South Los Angeles area, near the Museum of Natural History, because it was within walking distance of work; an administrative agency where I had been hired to fill in for an employee who was on maternity leave. The pay wasn't bad, so even though the place was nondescript, it was a lot better than the shack I'd lived in during my last stay in the city.

I sat on the couch, a glass of tea in my hand, my feet – in my brand new, extra-high, elegant, extra-tight pumps – on the coffee table, staring at the muted TV screen as I fiddled with the long, gold chain with colored semi-precious stones that Raff had given me when I graduated with a degree in Business Administration and Accounting.

"I like your necklace, Miss Brooks," I heard in my head the high-pitched voice of Carla, the sprightly star of the school's end-of-year party, and my lips curled into a smile that widened as I remembered the words Vance had whispered in my ear back then, "It's the throat that necklace hangs from that I like."

It had been a memorable evening, and with the exception of a couple of kids who went blank for a few seconds in the middle of their respective dialogues, the show had run smoothly and been a great success. Indeed, Carla and John's waltz had had the audience on its feet, and as they bent in an elaborate bow to acknowledge such enthusiasm, I couldn't help but notice the latter's family – including his big brother – cheering wildly a few rows away.

Then it was my turn to receive heartfelt congratulations from parents and teachers, and for a few moments I almost felt transported back to my dressing room after a performance. Vance was at my side the whole time, his arm around my waist, and I didn't miss the envious looks from more than one of the women there. My friend Linda, the director, begged me for the umpteenth time to take over the school's dance department, and for the umpteenth time I was tempted to stop hesitating and accept the cowboy's proposal.

God, I missed him!

I took a sip of iced tea, lost in thought. I was very busy during the day, and except for occasional moments, I could control my homesickness, but at night I tossed and turned in bed until I finally fell asleep. More than once, though, I had woken up gasping for breath after dreaming of Vance running his tanned, long-fingered hands over every nook and cranny of my body.

At the urging of Hanna, a coworker I'd hit it off with from the start, we'd gone out for drinks after work a couple of times, but on both occasions I couldn't help but compare the men who'd approached us to Vance, and the truth was, they all came off very badly.

I sighed as I remembered the last few days at the Double B. Of course, the day after we got back, the cowboy accompanied me to the sheriff's office. I was very nervous, but I shouldn't have been. Although Tom gave Vance a good lecture for not bringing me in right away, he had been very nice to me throughout. As soon as I arrived, he had one of his men bring me coffee and patiently coaxed the information he wanted out of me. If I wasn't sure about something, Vance would help me out. After listening to his statement and mine, the sheriff told us not to worry because we probably wouldn't even have to testify in front of the judge. I sighed with relief; I had had enough 'judge's rulings' to last me a lifetime.

The worst thing happened when we walked out into the street. Suddenly, a middle-aged woman with wet cheeks and very red eyes came out to meet us.

"I'm sorry, I'm really sorry. I'm so sorry."

Surprised, I turned to Vance, not knowing what to say, but he had already put an arm around the woman's frail form, offering her comfort. "You don't have to be sorry, Nora. Nothing that has happened is your fault."

Then I realized that this stranger, who seemed to carry the weight of the world on her shoulders, must be Colin's mother. I was immediately overcome with infinite compassion, so I approached her and took her hands in mine.

"I am sorry for the loss of your son." And I didn't say it just for the sake of saying it. I've always thought that there is nothing more terrible than a mother losing a beloved child, even if that child was a monster.

We stayed with her until she calmed down a bit. Then we took her home and walked away in silence, holding hands.

The voice of the neighbor next door, who must have just come home from work, brought me back to the present. Startled, I looked at the clock again and jumped up. I'd better run if I didn't want to be late. I grabbed the small silk handbag and the only stylish coat I had and hurried out, putting it on on the way.

As luck would have it, I managed to hail a free cab outside the door, and just as I dropped breathlessly into a seat in the front rows of the Dorothy Chandler Pavilion, the golden lights of the theater dimmed and the first notes of Adolphe Adam's ballet score began to play. I immediately got goosebumps, and I don't think my skin returned to its normal state until the curtain came down for the last time.

I remembered other opening nights and other applause, and I couldn't help but get a lump in my throat. People began to put on their coats and leave, but I stayed for quite a while, unable to move. I put my hands to my face and realized that my cheeks were wet. However, they were not tears of sadness, but of deep emotion. The emotion of once again enjoying an art that had always fascinated me, even though I was no longer a part of it. Eric's performance had been masterful and I had to admit that his *Giselle* had been up to the task.

"Is something the matter, miss?" asked an elderly man walking down the aisle behind his wife.

"No, nothing, thank you." I shook my head with a smile and the man continued on his way.

I finally took a deep breath, now came the hardest part. I got up and walked to the dressing rooms without hesitation; I knew the way.

How I had missed the joy after the premiere. The dancers walking back and forth, talking and laughing loudly, toasting with champagne, their faces heavily made up and still dressed in the colorful costumes they had worn for the last act.

One of my former companions saw me at that moment, and the toast she was about to make stopped halfway through. Gradually, those closest to me turned around and unconsciously began to form an aisle down which I slowly made my way.

In the back, in front of one of the large dressing tables surrounded by lit bulbs, Eric and Antea, each holding a glass of champagne, were smiling and chatting with the dancer who had played the role of Hilarion. Antea was the first to notice my presence and her mouth fell open as if her jaw had been knocked out of joint. She looked really stupid and I was glad.

"Hello, Antea."

At the sound of my voice, Eric turned to me with a look of disbelief. "Aisha!"

"Hi, Eric." I was about to shake his hand, but it suddenly seemed ridiculous to use such a formal greeting with a man who had been my lover for years, so instead I took a step closer, leaned forward and kissed him on both cheeks. He smelled of the same cologne he'd been wearing since I'd met him, and it suddenly seemed like a cloying, artificial scent.

"You look… You look amazing." He looked me up and down, and I couldn't help but notice that his eyes lingered on my bad leg for a second longer than necessary.

"You look amazing too." It was true. Eric had always been a man of perfect features, so perfect that his beauty was somewhat effeminate.

I shook my head, surprised at such a reaction to a man I had until recently considered the embodiment of perfection. But it was true; next to Vance, Eric would look like a puny little girl. The image almost made me burst out laughing, and I had to bite my lip hard to control myself.

Eric's eyes narrowed as if he'd noticed my reaction. I guess he was more used to my former adoring expression. "Where have you been these past months? I've missed you."

Ha. Sure. Still, I enjoyed the murderous glint I caught in Antea's big blue eyes and gave her a honeyed smile. "I was in the country."

"In the country?" I realized that I had really surprised him. I think in all the time we'd spent together, our only contact with nature had been the occasional swim at Venice Beach.

"On a ranch in Wyoming."

"Awesome!"

"Surrounded by handsome cowboys, I imagine. How romantic." Antea's sarcasm amused me, though I don't think it did the same for Eric. He had pursed his lips in a pout of disgust that I knew all too well.

"Yes, very romantic. But I can assure you that in Wyoming, men are not only handsome, but also made of a different stuff. More… manly, so to speak." I knew I had hit a nerve. One of the things that pissed my ex-boyfriend off the most was that nearly everyone, as soon as they noticed his pretty face and found out he was a ballet dancer, automatically assumed he was gay.

"Aisha, my love, you look stunning!" Adam, a colleague with whom I had always gotten along well and who had been my shoulder to cry on many occasions, came over to give me a hug. "I think being away from us agrees with you."

"I think so too," I said with a dazzling smile. Adam winked at me, gave me a light kiss on the lips and walked off to chat with another group.

"But you came to stay, didn't you?" Eric reached out and took my hand, but I let go immediately. "I'm not lying when I say I missed you. I haven't laughed like I did when we were together in ages"

"Eric!" Antea's cheeks flushed with anger.

"Calm down." I raised my palms. "I didn't come here to make you two fight."

"Then why did you come here, if I may ask?"

"I simply came to congratulate you both on a fabulous performance," I said, unfazed by Antea's rudeness. "It's been a long time since I've enjoyed a ballet, and I really appreciate it."

Eric kept his eyes on me.

"You look different." He suddenly narrowed his eyes and asked bluntly, "Are you seeing someone?"

The obvious jealousy in his voice didn't go to my head. Eric had always been a very possessive man and couldn't bear the thought of losing even one of his admirers. Again I was struck by the unkind thought. It was as if I had just had cataract surgery and my ex-boyfriend's figure had regained its sharpness. Only it wasn't the outside that I saw, but what was inside. Suddenly I could tell the true from the false, I was no longer blind where he was concerned.

"Well, I have met someone." My laconic answer didn't reveal much, but I wasn't going to use what bound me to Vance to make an ex jealous. To do so would be to devalue all that had happened between us.

"Aisha," Eric took my hand in his again, "I apologize, I was not up to the task, but there is still time to rebuild what was between us."

Maybe I should have been happy about this little triumph, even though I knew for a fact that he was just saying it to prove to himself that he still had some power over me, but all I felt was pity for the woman standing next to me, humiliated by his comments, unable to respond.

"I think you should apologize to Antea." Eric looked at me startled, as if he had completely forgotten that his current girlfriend was there, and I remembered that my ex was capable of taking his self-centeredness to unimaginable extremes. "There's nothing to rebuild between us. I realize now that there was never much of anything. Just a poor, stupid girl who worshipped you and a ballet star who let himself be worshipped."

"Apparently you didn't worship me enough. The proof is that it didn't take you long to find someone else. You swore to me you would never love anyone like me."

I sighed deeply and looked at him with the patience a mother shows a spoiled child who is about to throw a tantrum. "Anyway, there's no point in dwelling on the past."

I released the hand he still held between his, rested my palms on his shoulders and looked into his eyes. It seemed strange not to have to stand on tiptoe. I had almost forgotten that he was only half an inch taller than me.

"I don't think we'll see each other again, Eric. This is also a goodbye. I have felt the need to say goodbye to you for a long time, to put the past behind me once and for all." I leaned over and kissed him again on both cheeks. "Goodbye, I wish you a happy life."

Eric did not return my good wishes.

"I don't understand how, after all this," he made a sweeping gesture with his arms, "you can settle for some hick from Wyoming." But his spiteful remark didn't bother me at all.

"If you were a woman, you'd understand, believe me. Thank God Vance isn't a dancer." I let out a mischievous chuckle. "If he had to put on ballet tights, I assure you there wouldn't be a woman in the audience who could concentrate on the choreography." With that parting shot, I turned and left the dressing room without looking back.

18

Back in my apartment, I kicked off my shoes with a sigh of relief and threw them across the tiny living room. Limping a little, I opened the freezer, pulled out a tub of ice cream, and plopped down on the couch. With my legs up on the coffee table, I began to eat spoonfuls of ice cream, still thinking about what had happened.

After the initial adrenaline rush following the confrontation with Eric, I had run out of steam. Wasn't it depressing to have suffered so much for a man who didn't deserve it? I almost wished I had not shattered the rose-colored glasses through which I used to look at my ex. It was not a pleasant feeling to feel like the protagonist of a cheap melodrama.

I shoved another spoonful of ice cream into my mouth and swallowed it down, barely tasting it. The sound of the phone startled me and I almost dropped the spoon. I reached into my purse and pulled out my cell phone.

It was Raff from Madrid. He called to tell me that he had just become a father. He sounded euphoric and spoke very fast. He made me promise that as soon as I had a few days, I would visit them and meet my nephew. He would take the opportunity to introduce me to India, his wife, and Sol, their daughter, whom my brother also seemed to adore. We talked for a few more minutes, and when I hung up, I felt even more blue.

I shoved another spoonful of ice cream into my mouth. It wasn't that I wasn't happy for Raff. My brother was an extraordinary man, and he more than deserved all the good things that happened to him. It was just that…

Now it was the sound of the doorbell that pulled me out of my gloomy thoughts. I looked at the kitchen clock, it was almost eleven o'clock at night. I frowned and thought that maybe my neighbor had gotten sick and his wife needed me to take care of their little girl while they went to the hospital.

Still holding the tub of ice cream, I ran to the door and opened it. "Did something happen to…?"

I stopped, speechless. It wasn't the neighbor.

"Do you always open the door without asking who it is? What if I was a rapist or a serial killer?"

With his arms on his hips and his Stetson pulled low over his forehead, Vance looked at me disapprovingly.

I squeezed my eyelids tightly shut and opened them again in case I had fallen asleep and was dreaming.

"So, can I come in?"

"But... it's... it's not fall yet." I stammered, not knowing what I was saying, as he pulled me aside to come in.

"You see, I was just passing by..."

This was so patently untrue that a silly laugh escaped me as I continued to stare at him, my hands almost frozen, clenched around the tub of ice cream. I still couldn't believe he was real.

Vance looked me up and down, and judging by the way those green eyes sparkled, I think he liked what he saw.

"Did you get all dressed up to eat that for dinner?" He pointed at the ice cream.

"I just got back from the ballet."

He stood very still and said nothing, but I didn't pay too much attention. I was still trying to recover from the shock of seeing him in the middle of my living room, his size further dwarfing the tiny dimensions of my apartment.

"Aren't you going to kiss me?" Was I really begging? Pathetic.

I had fantasized a hundred times about what would happen when we met again, and in none of my fantasies had our reunion come close.

Vance tipped his hat back a little. I'd rarely seen him so serious, but all I could think about was how much I'd missed him and how gorgeous he looked.

"You're back with Eric?"

I didn't even hear what he asked me. I put the tub of ice cream down on the table with a thud and walked over to him. Tiptoeing, I grabbed the hat from him and threw it in the same place the shoes had gone with a quick flick of my wrist. Satisfied, I stood on tiptoe again and dug my fingers into the thick dark hair at his nape.

"If you won't, I will."

And I kissed him.

And he kissed me back.

And then I realized how blind I had been.

It was him, Vance Bennet, the man I was in love with. A true love: mature and balanced. One where it wasn't one person giving everything and the other taking it like it was their right.

I was sure that our life together would not be a bed of roses. That we would often fight, that his self-control would often get on my nerves, after all, he was the most unflappable guy in the world, while I was like a firebrand, igniting emotions and sparking action as soon as I got out of bed. But I had no doubt that he would always be there for me. He had more than proven it to me, and in that moment, I vowed that I would always be there for him, too.

"Vance, Vance, Vance," I murmured against his lips, still stroking his hair. "I can't believe you're here tonight. I needed you so much."

He pulled me closer. "I couldn't go another minute without seeing you, Aisha. According to my sister, I've been insufferable these past few months. Josh runs away every time he sees me, Miguel makes about twenty impertinent comments a day, and even Fernanda hasn't hesitated to throw more than a hint at me."

I smiled with my mouth glued to his. "You know? Deep down, I liked her from the beginning. I confess, I've missed them all, including Fernanda."

Vance also smiled when he heard me, and we shared another heated kiss that raised the temperature in the apartment a few degrees.

"I wanted to have a serious talk with you first, but I'm afraid that will have to wait until later." The unmistakable note of desire in his voice made me shiver. "How the hell do you take this off?" Impatiently he tugged at the zipper of my dress.

"Easy, cowboy." I reached behind my back to help him and let the dress fall to my feet.

I heard him gasp at the sight of the black lace ensemble I was wearing underneath and smiled with delight at his next comment, which actually sounded more like an impatient grunt.

"Our talk will definitely have to wait until much, much later." He bent down, slipped one arm behind my knees and lifted me into the air. I clung to his neck, buried my face in his throat and inhaled the familiar clean smell with delight.

Once again I had been completely wrong.

The reunion had been unlike any I had fantasized about since leaving the Double B. This reunion was, and promised to be, a thousand times better.

One more summer

"Have you seen Josh?"

Without waiting for an answer, Sol, India and Raff's daughter, ran past me like an exhalation in the direction of the barn. The sight of this miniature cowgirl running away with the two blonde braids flying behind her made me laugh.

Ever since she had arrived at the Double B, she had clung to Josh like a limpet, announcing to anyone who would listen that she was going to marry him when she grew up. Of course, that announcement had unleashed a barrage of jokes that poor Josh had endured with admirable fortitude, and of course, the task of teaching her to ride had fallen to him. Fortunately, Vance's brother had a sense of humor as well as infinite patience, and in just two weeks the sprightly little Spaniard was riding as if she had spent her entire life on horseback.

After his unexpected appearance at the door of my Los Angeles apartment, Vance had no trouble convincing me that we should get married as soon as possible.

I think the scales definitely tipped in his favor when he told me that Tessa had announced that she was marrying a well-known Jackson Hole businessman and would be moving there after the wedding. Of course, Josh and Carol would be staying at the Double B, so the arrangement sounded fantastic to me.

As I had told her stepson, very proud of my insight, "I thought all that back and forth to Jackson was suspicious." To which he had responded by rolling his eyes before giving me one of those kisses that had the virtue of making me look like a complete idiot.

Or maybe I'd agreed to marry him because there weren't many people who could resist that stubborn, bossy cowboy when he got something into his head.

Or maybe it was because he made love to me for hours until I couldn't even think.

The truth was that two weeks later we were married at the Doble B, in an intimate and perfect ceremony, in which none of Fernanda's pessimistic predictions came true, as she kept complaining that with so little time to prepare, the whole wedding would be a botch.

Raff flew in from New York to be my best man, and a few days later we began the incredible honeymoon that took us all over Europe, the first stop being Madrid, where I met

India, Sol, and little Rafa, and where I fell in love three times over.

Now it was my brother's whole family, who had flown to Wyoming to spend a few weeks at the Double B, taking advantage of school vacation. That morning I had offered to stay with the adorable Rafa so that India and Raff could go for a long ride, and from the hungry looks my brother gave her all the time and the adoring ones she gave him back, I had no doubt that they were going to do more than just admire the view. Something I could easily understand, as I too was counting the days until Vance and I could have our secret meadow all to ourselves again.

I felt like little orphan Annie when she sang, "The sun will come out. Tomorrow." No matter how many times I had lost hope, the sun had risen again in my life. My passion for ballet had found an outlet in the dance classes at Wilson High School, and now I could share all the love I felt for dance. And to top it all off, there were those Saturday nights when my husband and I would go to a dance hall in Jackson. Can you imagine anything sexier than dancing a tango with the hottest cowboy in town?

At that moment, little Rafa started to squeal and I looked down at him and smiled. "And what do you think, Rafa? Will Sol get away with it? My money's on her."

The chubby baby on my hip caught a strand of my hair with a drooling fist and babbled animatedly.

"Is that a yes?" I leaned down to kiss his soft rosy cheeks and sniffed his scent with delight.

"It seems so."

I looked up to find Vance standing before me in his characteristic pose: legs slightly apart, thumbs hooked into the belt loops of his pants, hat pulled back a little. I hadn't expected to see him that morning, knowing that he and the rest of the men on the ranch were busy preparing to move the cattle to the summer pastures.

It was quite hot and he had rolled up the sleeves of his blue shirt to his elbows, exposing his tanned forearms. The worn and dusty jeans accentuated his long legs and that hard, shapely butt, which, although I couldn't see it from this angle, was the kind that made you salivate at the sight of it. In short, my favorite cowboy was a walking ad for the Wild West, where virile and dangerous men abounded.

"Hello, cowboy," I whispered provocatively.

"Hello, princess." His eyes smiled.

Rafa tugged hard on my hair and I was forced to pay attention to him. "That's not okay, *señorito*." I let go of my hair and blew a raspberry kiss on his chubby cheek, drawing an infectious laugh from him.

"You know," Vance said. "I've never seen anything more flattering on you."

I looked down in surprise. I was wearing the same pink shirt I'd worn hundreds of times and my favorite jeans, so worn the fabric threatened to rip at the knees.

"These old jeans?"

"No, that little blue-eyed guy."

Then I raised my face to his again and our eyes locked. The corners of his eyes formed those familiar little wrinkles, and a slow smile pulled at my lips. And there was no need to say more, for we both knew that this silent exchange held a wonderful promise.

Thank you for reading

The Sun Rises in the West

I sincerely hope you've enjoyed it.
For more information about the release of upcoming books and stories,
sign up for my newsletter at:
www.isabelkeats.com
(you will only receive notices regarding the publication of new works),
follow me on Twitter @IsabelKeats,
or like my fan page.
Facebook
Reader reviews help others discover my work.
I therefore welcome your opinion of what you've just read, be it positive or negative.

Would you like to see any other of the books I've written translated into your language?
If so, feel free to contact me at isabelkeats@gmail.com

Other books in English by this author

More than neighbors

When Leopold Sinclair returned from a long overseas business trip, the last thing he expected to find was a sexy new tenant in the apartment next door. Catalina Stapleton, the beautiful, recently arrived neighbor, is the type of person who just can't help adopting every poor stray she comes across. After a brief exchange with her uptight and work-obsessed neighbor, she decides that Leopold is an unhappy man who needs to be saved from himself.

Yet soon, what started as her friendly project turns personal. After a red-hot kiss inflames their attraction, Leopold knows he must keep wild Cat at a distance or risk bringing down the barriers he's worked so hard to maintain. Determined to protect their blossoming friendship, each hides their growing romantic feelings – and nearly overwhelming desires. But how long will they be able to keep up the façade?

Skinny legs

What would you do if the boy who had picked on you in grammar school suddenly reentered your life as a dashing heartthrob in need of your help? Would you settle old scores or try to forgive and forget?

A Christmas short story with a romantic twist!

Black Wolf

For as long as Taima can remember, her life has never been a bed of roses. Growing up as an orphan among the Nei Me tribe means hard work, little food and cruel punishments, but all that is about to change. The black wolf of her dreams has come to the rescue. Zane Wade, a former Union soldier turned bounty hunter, is a dangerous man who has lost faith in humanity. His only ambition is to use the money he has saved up over the years to buy some land and start a cattle ranch. The last thing he imagines when he rescues a young woman from the clutches of some bandits is that she will radically change both his life and the way he sees the world.

A dangerous cowboy, a remarkable young woman... Don't miss this extraordinary tale of passionate love set in the Wild West!

About the author

Isabel Keats is just an ordinary woman who one day felt like writing. A mother of a large family (dog included), she is lucky to have something more valuable than gold: free time, even if not as much as she'd like. She loves romance and loves happy endings, so in short, she writes romance because at this point in her life it's what she most wants to read.

Isabel Keats – winner of the HQÑ Digital Prize with ***Empezar de nuevo*** (*Starting Again*), shortlisted for the first Harlequín Short Story Prize with her novel ***El protector*** (*The Protector*) and for the third Vergara-RNR Romantic Novel Contest with ***Abraza mi oscuridad*** (*Embrace My Darkness*) – is the pseudonym concealing a graduate in advertising from Madrid, a wife, and a mother of three girls. To date she has published almost two dozen works, including novels and short stories.

Learn more about this author at:
www.isabelkeats.com

Made in United States
Cleveland, OH
21 November 2024

10846204R00166